Praise for *Amanda in France*

"Revisiting Paris with Amanda was a roller-coaster ride through the city I once knew so well. A great adventure story, and I couldn't put it down!"
— Maureen Moss, author of *The Tour Guide Life - It Could be Yours, More to Life* and *There's a Funnelweb on the Floor!*

"Amanda's latest romp around the world's favourite city of love will appeal to both the armchair traveller and the mystery fan."
— Gina McMurchy-Barber,
Author of *The Jigsaw Puzzle King*
(Winner of the 2021 Silver Birch Awards)

"Children all over the world, impatiently waiting for this latest addition to your *Amanda Travels* series, will not be disappointed!"
— Marion Iberg

"I found the book compelling in the way a tragic news story has been woven into a mystery for children. Readers will want to explore more about the famous cathedral after reading this book."
—Sheila MacArthur

The **Amanda Travels** Series:

Amanda in Arabia: The Perfume Flask

Amanda in Spain: The Girl in the Painting

Amanda in England: The Missing Novel

Amanda in Alberta: The Writing on the Stone

Amanda on the Danube: The Sounds of Music

Amanda in New Mexico: Ghosts in the Wind

Amanda in Holland: Missing in Action

Amanda in Malta: The Sleeping Lady

Amanda in France: Fire in the Cathedral

AMANDA
IN
FRANCE
FIRE IN THE CATHEDRAL

DARLENE FOSTER

central
avenue
PUBLISHING

2022

Published by Central Avenue Publishing, an imprint of Central Avenue Marketing Ltd.
www.centralavenuepublishing.com

Published in Canada
Printed in United States of America

AMANDA IN FRANCE: FIRE IN THE CATHEDRAL

978-1-77168-274-9 pbk

1. JUVENILE FICTION/Travel 2. JUVENILE FICTION / People & Places - Europe

To
Marie Mehrer
1948 – 2022
a special Amanda fan

I

Amanda looked up—way up. In front of her a massive wrought-iron lattice structure pierced the brilliant blue morning sky.

"Wow! The Eiffel Tower! It's even more amazing in real life."

"Unreal, isn't it?" Leah shaded her eyes with her hand.

"Can we go up to the top?" asked Amanda.

"Not today, but maybe later," replied Leah's Aunt Jenny.

Amanda's eyes glowed with gratitude as she placed her hand on her chest. "Thanks for inviting me to join you both here in France."

"I figure that's the least we could do after you came all the way to Malta to help us. I'm pleased you could get time off from school."

Amanda loved listening to Aunt Jenny's Scottish accent.

"When I told my teacher we would be sleeping in a bookstore, she was all for it. I just need to hand in a writing project when I get back."

"At least we can relax and enjoy Paris. We won't be chased by bad guys or have to look for lost artifacts." Leah grinned. "And the shopping here is fabulous."

They took selfies with Monsieur Eiffel's iconic tower behind them and then caught the crowded Metro. "This is our stop," said Aunt Jenny after a few minutes. They climbed up steep stairs, dodging passengers in a hurry to get to their destinations, and emerged onto a tree-lined street. Four lanes of crazy traffic flew by in each direction.

"This is the Avenue des Champs-Élysées, the most famous street in Paris and an important thoroughfare," announced Aunt Jenny. "Follow me." She led them past high-end shops with the latest fashions adorning some windows and glittering jewellery in others. "You can buy anything you want here." She stopped in front of a store with a red Lamborghini sports car in the window. "As long as you have the money!"

Amanda pointed to a huge stone archway at the far end of the street. "What is that?"

"The Arc de Triomphe, the heart of Paris," Aunt Jenny replied. "Twelve avenues spread out from the circular plaza making it look like it is the centre of a star. Come, let's get a picture of you in front of it, Amanda."

They crossed the hectic street and stopped at a narrow divider in the middle. Amanda's heart raced as cars and motor scooters whipped around her on both sides.

"This is the very best place to take a selfie with the Arc behind you."

"Yikes!" Amanda shuddered. "Is it safe?"

"Sort of. Others are doing it too. But be quick as there is a queue."

Amanda noticed a line of tourists waiting to stand where

she stood, on a concrete island in the middle of a busy street. She forced a smile as Leah held out the camera and took a selfie of them in front of the famous attraction.

When they reached the other side of the street, Amanda took a breath. "Now that was insane."

"Never a dull moment with Aunt Jenny." Leah rolled her eyes.

Two teenage boys, dressed in old-fashioned clothing decorated with gold *fleurs-de-lys*, handed out pamphlets near the Arc.

"*Mademoiselle*, would you like to see a play at the Opera House?" asked one boy as he placed a pamphlet in Amanda's hand.

She smiled. "Thank you. I mean, *merci*."

His face lit up. "Where are you from?"

"Canada."

"Then you must speak *le français*. Canada is a French-speaking country, *non*?"

"We are a bilingual country, and I'm learning French in school, so I know a little bit." She pointed to his costume. "I also learned that the *fleur-de-lys* is a lily and was a symbol of the kings of France."

"*Mais oui*! Welcome to Paris. Perhaps we will see you at the Opera House tonight. It is a most famous play, called *The Phantom of the Opera*. Perhaps you have heard of it?"

"Oh yes! I saw it in Calgary with my great-aunt Mary. I loved it."

"Show this coupon and you will get a discount. Tell them

Pierre sent you." He winked and moved on.

Amanda's face felt hot.

"I see you made a friend already." Leah smirked. "He sure is cute."

Under the Arc, a flat slab, outlined with copper bricks and a low chain border, caught Amanda's attention. A flame burned at one end. "What's that, over there with the red, white, and blue flowers around it?"

"That is the Tomb of the Unknown Soldier," answered Aunt Jenny. "It honours the thousands of French soldiers whose final resting place is not known. The eternal flame is never put out and is rekindled every evening at 6:30."

Amanda moved closer to get a better look. She placed her hand over her heart and sniffled as she thought of her great-uncle who had been in World War II. She only recently learned that he was buried in Holland. Thinking about war always made her sad.

Lost in thought, she bumped into a man crouched down on his knees, taking pictures.

"I'm so sorry."

He looked over his shoulder and shrugged. "No problem." The man stood up, towering over her, and nodded before walking to the other side of the memorial. His salt-and-pepper hair was pulled back in a long ponytail, and she noticed he walked with a slight limp.

"So, what are we going to do next?" she asked Leah.

"If we can get Aunt Jenny away from those carvings on the side of the Arc, maybe we can go shopping! I love shopping in Paris much more than shopping back home in London."

Amanda looked back and saw that the man had his camera aimed right at Leah's aunt.

❀ ❀ ❀

After they visited some shops and bought chic red berets, Aunt Jenny led them to a bookstore called Shakespeare and Company. "This is where we'll be staying for the next few nights," she announced.

A friendly young man opened the front door for them. Rows and rows of books, displayed on two levels lined with shelves, begged to be read. Amanda breathed in the welcoming smell of books, old and new. Her heart wanted to burst.

"This has got to be my happy place!" She ran over to a shelf and pulled out a copy of *Anne of Green Gables*. "This is my most favourite book of all."

A store clerk with bright red hair and black-rimmed glasses joined her. "That is a very popular book, even though it was written a long time ago. It's about a girl in Canada. Is that where you're from?"

"Yes." Amanda beamed. "But Anne Shirley is from Prince Edward Island, on the east coast, and I'm from Alberta, in the western part of the country."

"Are you here for the Tumbleweed program?"

"Yes, we all are," interjected Aunt Jenny. "I'm Jenny Anderson. This is my niece Leah Anderson and her friend, Amanda Ross."

"We've been expecting you. I'm Fiona, the manager, and I'll show you around. Let's go upstairs and put your backpacks away. I'm sure you are familiar with the rules, but just to be sure, you only need to work in the bookshop for a couple of hours each day. Make sure to write an autobiography for our files before you leave. Feel free to work on any of your own writing projects if you wish." She unlocked a door that opened to a set of stairs, which led to an attic room containing three sets of bunk beds and a desk. "I hope you don't mind sharing. The bathroom is through the door over there as well as a small kitchenette where you can make coffee or tea. Get settled in, then come downstairs and tell me what shifts you would like to work."

A briefcase and jacket lay on the bottom of one bunk.

Leah scrunched her eyebrows. She didn't look pleased. "You mean we have to share this room with other people?"

Amanda tugged at her arm. "Come on, this will be so much fun. Do you want the top or bottom bunk?"

Aunt Jenny placed her shawl and backpack on the bottom of another bunk. "Besides, I'll be here too. And it's only for a few nights. Amanda's right, it should be fun." She winked at Amanda.

Someone came out of the small kitchen with a cell phone to his ear and, without looking at them, walked down the stairs. His ponytail swung from side to side, and he walked with a slight limp.

Amanda's scalp prickled. *Could it be?* She shook her head. *No way.*

2

BACK DOWNSTAIRS THEY FOUND FIONA. LEAH ASKED, "DO WE have to sleep in that room with other people, like that man?"

"You mean Mr. Lawrence? He's leaving today. He may come back to do more research on his book but not to sleep. You three will have the place to yourselves tonight. A college student, Aimee, will join you tomorrow. We don't usually have people as young as you stay, but because you are here with Ms. Anderson, we decided it would be OK. Besides, Amanda wrote a compelling letter explaining her writing project and why she wanted to be part of the Tumbleweed program."

Amanda thrust her chest out and glowed. "Thank you for letting us stay in the store. Now, when can we get to work?"

Leah frowned and narrowed her eyes.

Fiona picked up a pile of books. "Amanda, why don't you put these books back on the shelves alphabetically in the Children and Young Adult section? That way you can familiarize yourself with the store in case someone needs help finding a book." She turned to Leah and smiled. "The vintage fashion magazine section is a mess. Could you please rearrange them by date? If there are some you would like to look through later, put them aside."

Aunt Jenny followed Fiona to the History and Archae-ology section on the second level. As Amanda put books back on the shelves, a little girl entered the store with a well-dressed woman. "I wonder where the Paddington Bear books are, Mummy."

Amanda turned and pointed to a nearby shelf. "The Paddington Bear books are right over there." A relaxed smile crossed her face; she was pleased to be able to help someone so soon. She knew she would love working in this bookstore.

After a while, Aunt Jenny came down the stairs with her arms full of books. "I'm going to take these to our room for research later. Then we'll go for something to eat and maybe visit the cathedral."

❦ ❦ ❦

The sun was still shining when they left the store and wandered over a metal bridge to an island in the middle of the city. Amanda sniffed the air. Paris smelled different than other cities she had visited. The scent was a blend of coffee, cigarette smoke, and perfume mixed with the faint sour smell of old drains.

She looked down the river and noticed a number of bridges spanning the water. "This is such a pretty river. It looks like a painting. What is it called?"

Aunt Jenny replied, "Why, it's the Seine. A very famous river, painted by many artists over the years." She pointed to a cathedral towering over leafy trees in the distance.

"There's Notre-Dame. Should we go there first?"

"You mean like—from *The Hunchback of Notre-Dame*?" Amanda's heart quickened.

"The one and the same." Aunt Jenny grinned.

Leah rolled her eyes. "Yes, and he may still be there haunting the church."

As they neared the imposing building, Aunt Jenny became excited. "There isn't much of a queue, let's go inside now."

"But—I'm hungry," said Leah.

"We won't be long."

"I would really like to see the inside," replied Amanda as she stared at the two grand towers bordering a large door.

The entire façade was covered in carvings. Above the door, a round stained-glass window sparkled in the sun. A group of students in school uniforms emerged from the cathedral. Strains of organ music drifted out the open door. The line moved up quickly and they were soon inside the massive stone structure. Amanda felt incredibly small as her eyes followed the many carved arches meeting at a point in the high vaulted ceiling. She stared at the huge organ pipes and felt the vibrations of the music in her bones. A choir began to sing, filling the building with an exquisite melody. Amanda stood mesmerized as stained-glass windows created a kaleidoscope of colours that danced to the music.

"Amanda, come on, let's go." Leah tugged at her arm.

"This has got to be the most amazing church I've ever visited. I'm definitely writing about it in my school report," exclaimed Amanda as they left the building. She looked up at the many carvings on the front of the church, splashed with sunshine. "Those figures are awesome."

"They illustrate biblical stories," explained Aunt Jenny. "In medieval days, the cathedral was called a poor people's book for the churchgoers, who were mostly illiterate. It was a way for them to be able to learn the stories from the Bible."

"That's fascinating." Amanda pointed up to grotesque creatures peering down at them. "And what are those? I don't think they're from Bible stories."

"Those are gargoyles. They serve as decorative rain-spouts, preserving the stone walls by causing the water to flow away from them. I've been doing research on them recently."

"Why are they so scary looking?"

"It was a medieval marketing trick. They're supposed to represent the horrors of living a wicked life, encouraging people to come inside and be rescued." Aunt Jenny grinned. "Now let's stop blethering and get a bite to eat."

Amanda zoomed in with her camera and took pictures of the scary open-mouthed creatures, some with horns and wings, and all with fearsome faces. *I wouldn't want to meet one of those in the night.* She shivered.

As she moved her camera around, a tall man with a long ponytail came into view. He was also taking pictures, but not of gargoyles. His camera was focused on Aunt Jenny.

Amanda felt a shiver go through her.

They sat outside and enjoyed a salad with cheese-stuffed baguettes at the Quasimodo Café across the street from Notre-Dame. As they munched on sweet macarons for dessert, the bells of the cathedral rang out.

Amanda envisioned the hunchback ringing the bells. "I so love this place. Paris just might be my favourite place in the whole world."

Leah punched her on the shoulder. "You say that about every place we visit."

A brown-skinned girl with corn braids stopped by their table. "Pardon, are you Madame Anderson?" she addressed Aunt Jenny.

"Yes, yes I am."

"I am Aimee Mbaye. Fiona has sent me to find you. Someone has gone through your belongings at the bookstore."

The older woman paled. "Oh, no. I thought it was safe to leave our things there."

They quickly paid for the meal and raced back to the store.

"I'm so sorry," apologized Fiona. "I was sure the door to the upstairs rooms was locked. When Aimee came to put her backpack in the room, we noticed your stuff scattered about."

Aunt Jenny checked her backpack and put everything back into it. "It's odd that nothing is missing, even my tablet is still here." She glanced at the bed where her research books lay neatly arranged. "It's as if someone displayed them to take a picture." She shook her head.

"My things are all here too," said Leah.

"I don't think I have anything missing either." Amanda looked under the bed. "Who'd do this? What could they have been looking for?"

Leah scowled. "It was probably that guy that was staying here."

3

THAT NIGHT AMANDA TOSSED AND TURNED. SHE DREAMT THE hunchback was chasing her through Notre-Dame, but when he caught her, he became the man with the ponytail. She woke up trembling.

At breakfast, Aunt Jenny decided the girls should work in the bookstore while she did research. After lunch, they could go sightseeing.

Leah moaned, "I don't really want to work in the bookshop. Can't we go shopping instead?"

"The picture book section is a mess. I can't wait to tidy it up." Amanda rubbed her hands together. "Plus I love helping people find books, especially the little kids. Yesterday, a mother came in with three children and I found a perfect book for each of them. They're from Australia and are living here for a year. How cool is that?"

"The next time someone asks me where a book is, I'll send them to you," said Leah with a smirk.

"Leah, you could at least try to enjoy this experience." Aunt Jenny gave a frustrated shake of her head and went upstairs.

✿ ✿ ✿

Amanda stood back and admired the neat and tidy section. Her tummy rumbled. She looked at the large clock on the wall and was surprised to see it was twelve o'clock already.

Fiona glanced over at her. "Those books haven't been so organized in a long time. Thanks, Amanda. You should stop for a break. Leah is already outside at the coffee shop."

Amanda joined her friend and they each had a croissant and a *café au lait* while waiting for Aunt Jenny. "Who was that boy in the black leather jacket I saw you chatting with?" she asked.

Leah shrugged. "Um, that was Jerome. He was waiting for his mother to find a book and was bored. He works part-time at a scooter repair shop and plays in a goth band."

Just then Aunt Jenny joined them. "Ready to look around? Let's go to Place des Vosges. It's interesting, and there are some great shops and restaurants."

"Is it far?" asked Leah.

"No. About a twenty-minute walk."

They crossed a stone bridge Aunt Jenny said was called Pont Neuf, which she explained meant New Bridge. She laughed. "In spite of its name, it is the oldest bridge in Paris and has an amazing history."

Amanda noticed a busker wearing yellow jeans and a red sweater, playing a guitar, and singing in the middle of the bridge. She giggled at the small black poodle sitting on his shoulder and dropped a few coins into the open case. When the musician doffed his fedora, she was startled to see the same man who had been staying at Shakespeare and Company, his long grey hair hanging loose.

"*Merci beaucoup*," he said and winked.

Her scalp prickled. *Why does he keep showing up?*

They reached a large picturesque square surrounded by red-brick buildings. People strolled the paths and picnicked on the lush green grass. On the ground floor of the buildings, stone arches covered the sidewalks. Aunt Jenny led them past many shops, art galleries, and restaurants under vaulted cathedral-like coverings. She stopped at Café Hugo.

"This is my favourite place. It's such a nice day, let's sit outside and have lunch."

Amanda's heart raced. "Oh, let's!" She looked up at the red-brick and white-stone arches that met at a decorative keystone in the middle. "This place is awesome!"

Aunt Jenny laughed. "It was built by a king a long time ago. They used to hold jousting tournaments on the grounds. The king and his court would sit under these arches, out of the sun, while being entertained."

Amanda envisioned knights in shining armour racing toward each other with their lances pointing, the crowd cheering them on. She jumped when Leah swatted her arm.

"Amanda, stop daydreaming and decide what you'd like for lunch."

"Oh, sorry." Amanda looked at the menu. "The *croque-madame* sounds good. It's like a grilled cheese and ham sandwich with béchamel sauce and a fried egg on top. I'll have that."

15

Aunt Jenny nodded. "Good choice."

"Café Hugo . . . is it named after the author of *The Hunchback of Notre-Dame*?" asked Amanda as her lunch was placed in front of her.

The waiter replied, "*Mai oui, mademoiselle.*" He pointed. "Monsieur Hugo lived in the apartments in that corner and wrote some of his famous books there. Have you read *Les Misérables*?"

"No. Is it good?"

"It is the best!" The waiter grinned from ear to ear.

Amanda took a bite of her *croque-madame*. "This is so scrummy."

After the delicious lunch, the girls enjoyed looking in the shops and art galleries. Amanda stopped to take pictures of the apartment the famous author had lived in, while Leah and her aunt checked out a clothing boutique. A small black poodle raced past her, almost knocking her down. Amanda looked around but couldn't see anyone following the dog. She hoped it wasn't lost. The dog ran over the grass and around a fountain, chasing a bird.

A man shouted, "Fifi, get back here. Right now!"

The dog's ears perked up. Looking around, she shook her head and bounded over to a man wearing yellow jeans and a fedora, who put her on a leash.

Amanda recognized the man immediately. She straightened her shoulders and marched over to him. "I'm glad you found your dog."

"Fifi has a habit of running off, especially if there are

birds around." He chuckled and rubbed the dog's head.

"Why do I feel like you're following us?" asked Amanda. "I saw you at the Arc de Triomphe, the bookstore, Notre-Dame, and then on the bridge. It looked like you were taking pictures of my friend's aunt."

"But I'm not following you. It's just a coincidence that I'm at the same places you are. Perhaps we have the same interests." He shrugged. "I need to take Fifi back home. I might see you again at the bookstore. I'm writing a book and need to do some research."

"Really. What is your book about?"

"Just crime drama. I'm not likely to be the next Victor Hugo." His eyes drifted across the square. "I better get going. Come along, Fifi." He walked briskly toward a statue of a king on a horse, just as someone in a black jacket disappeared behind it.

Leah arrived clutching a colourful shopping bag. "You will never believe the fab outfit I just bought. Who were you talking to?"

"A man with a dog. It's weird, he keeps showing up wherever we are."

"I'm sure it's nothing. Don't start looking for trouble, Amanda. Please! This is Paris. The city of love." Leah made a heart with her fingers.

4

AT THE ENTRANCE TO A METAL BRIDGE THEY WERE ABOUT TO cross, Amanda asked, "What are these?" She pointed to a garbage can with padlocks attached around the rim.

"Up until recently, it was a modern custom for lovers to attach love locks, with their names written on them, onto the side of this bridge, called Pont des Arts. Then they would throw the keys into the river below," explained Aunt Jenny. "It represented the couple's commitment to each other. The custom grew so popular that the weight of all the padlocks became a serious safety concern. Eventually a section of the bridge's side collapsed under the weight of them. As you can see, now the sides of the bridge are covered in Plexiglas so nothing can be attached. I guess a few couples have decided to use the rubbish bins to lock their love!"

"That's too bad. I like the idea of the love locks," replied Amanda.

"I told you, Paris is the city of loooove." Leah made a silly grin. "Look, down there on the quai, there are people having a picnic. Now that's sweet."

Amanda looked down at the wide stone walkway hugging the river. A table, covered in a linen cloth, was set with china, and around it sat two couples on folding chairs, laughing as they sipped their wine. An open bottle sat in the centre of the table. Beside them, on the ground, a large wicker basket rested with a baguette sticking out. The sun bounced off the water and illuminated the bridge near them.

Amanda took a picture. "That is the most romantic picnic I have ever seen."

"Only in Paris," said Aunt Jenny with a smile.

❋ ❋ ❋

When they returned to Shakespeare and Company, Aimee glanced up from dusting shelves. "Oh, there you are. Two young men stopped by and dropped off tickets to *The Phantom of the Opera* for you tonight."

Leah's face clouded over. "I don't want to see a boring old opera."

"It's not really an opera. It's a musical and it's a great love story. You'll enjoy it!" Amanda beamed. "Oh, please let's go."

"To see the play in the actual Paris Opera House would be a treat," agreed Aunt Jenny.

"And you can wear your new outfit." Amanda pointed to the bag in Leah's hand.

"I guess it would be good to see the inside of the opera house."

"There are four tickets, so if you wouldn't mind, I'd love to come along with you," said Aimee as she folded up her dustcloth.

"Of course. Please join us," replied Aunt Jenny.

Amanda zipped up her purple raincoat. A slight drizzle began as they headed toward the large imposing building that was the famous Paris Opera House. As they got closer, she could see the exterior covered with many sculptures. Every bit of space was decorated. The busts of well-known composers looked down from between stately marble columns. On the right and left corner of the façade stood huge golden-winged figures, glistening in the rain. Aunt Jenny said they were called Poetry and Harmony.

Once inside the main hall, Amanda stood with her mouth open. The room glittered with gold. Huge crystal chandeliers hung from the ceiling. Marble statues lined two magnificent staircases. She felt like she had entered wonderland.

Leah poked her. "Look up!"

Amanda bent her head back and gasped. "This place is unbelievable." The ceiling, painted with bright colours, looked like a spring garden.

"It is *magnifique*, is it not?" A familiar-looking young man wearing an usher's uniform stood beside her.

"Do you not remember me? I am Pierre. I saw you at the Arc de Triomphe." He grinned. "And you are the lovely Mademoiselle Amanda, from Canada. I am pleased you received the tickets I dropped off at the bookstore."

Amanda felt her face get red. She stammered, "Well—I—thank you!"

"You are early. Can I show you and your friends around the opera house before the play begins?"

Leah jumped in. "That would be great."

"You two go ahead," said Aunt Jenny. "Aimee and I will wait here, by the staircase. I want to get a better look at these statues."

Pierre took the girls backstage and pointed out the dressing rooms. He then took them to a door that led to the side of the stage. Amanda gulped as she looked out at the huge theatre full of red velvet seats, gold trimmings, and chandeliers.

"Wowza! This is wickedly posh," exclaimed Leah.

Leading the girls down some stairs behind the stage, he showed them the lake under the building.

"I remember this from the play," said Amanda.

"There really is one, and here it is," explained Pierre.

Amanda shivered and looked around, half expecting the phantom to appear.

When they arrived back upstairs, they encountered a huge commotion. Police directed people out the front door, where soldiers waited in a line.

Pierre stopped another usher rushing by. "What is going on?" he asked.

"Someone called the *gendarme* to say there was a bomb in the opera house." The young man's voice trembled. "We are trying to evacuate the building."

"A bomb!" Leah grabbed Amanda's hand. "Let's get out of here—fast!"

"Wait! It is too crowded. You will get crushed. I know another way." Pierre turned and walked briskly down a hallway.

Leah's eyes grew wide. "Should we follow him?"

"I think so," Amanda barely whispered as she gripped her friend's hand.

Pierre briskly led them down hallways, around corners, and through doors. The girls sprinted to keep up with him. Amanda hoped he knew where he was going. She sure didn't want to stay in the opera house if there was a bomb in it. Her heart beat faster and her throat felt dry.

Pierre tried a door but it was locked. "*Non!*" He threw his hands up in the air, then pointed. "We will try this way." He turned around and marched down another corridor. At the end loomed a large door with a sign in French and English: FIRE EXIT. USE ONLY IN AN EMERGENCY.

Pierre shrugged. "This is an emergency, *n'est-ce pas?*"

He pushed with all his weight against the door. It flew open. An alarm pierced their ears.

Outside, sirens filled the air as theatregoers in their finery spilled out of the front door. People shouted and ran every which way. One woman was crying, her mascara running down her face.

"Now how will we find Aunt Jenny and Aimee?" Leah bit her lip.

Amanda's eyes searched the crowd. She noticed a familiar-looking tall man with a ponytail, helping a police officer guide people away from the front door. Soldiers moved toward the entrance of the building.

"That will be *l'équipe de déminage*, the bomb disposal unit." Pierre clenched and unclenched his fists as he took a couple of shallow breaths. "We should move away from here, just in case there is an explosion." He grabbed Amanda's elbow and led the girls across the street, dodging frantic people.

Amanda trembled. She suddenly wished she was back home in Canada.

5

"*Pardon mademoiselles*, but I really must get back to work," said Pierre. "I'm sure if you wait right here, your aunt will find you."

Amanda nodded and forced a smile. "Th-thanks. I guess we'll be OK."

Leah stood on tiptoes, surveying the crowd.

Pierre was about to cross the street when the tall man with a ponytail appeared. "Oh, Monsieur Lawrence, *s'il vous plaît*, can you help Amanda and Leah locate their aunt and Aimee?"

"But of course, I know where they are. Come with me." He motioned to the girls to follow him. He led them down the street and around a corner, where he waved at two women standing in front of Galeries Lafayette. "Here! I have them here," he shouted.

Aunt Jenny and Aimee rushed over to them. "We were so worried about you." Aunt Jenny smothered Amanda in an embrace.

Aimee clung to Leah. "We didn't know if we should stay inside and wait for you, but they insisted we leave the building."

"Thank you so much for finding them." Aunt Jenny was on the verge of tears.

"Yes, Philippe. Thank you," said Aimee.

"No problem. I'm just glad you found each other. Now I must go, as my help is needed. I'll see you tomorrow."

"How do you know each other?" asked Amanda as she watched the man called Philippe Lawrence hurry back to the opera house, limping slightly.

"He volunteers at Shakespeare and Company," replied Aimee.

"Let's try to make our way back," said Aunt Jenny. "I'm sorry the evening has been ruined for you girls."

"I think we should stay here until the crowd thins out. It's mayhem out there," said Aimee. "I think the girls would like to see the inside of Galeries Lafayette."

"Sure," Amanda mumbled.

Still shaken by the thought of being in a building with a bomb in it, she wasn't keen on seeing any other sights. But she followed the rest into the large building and past display cases of jewellery, scarves, and perfume. *This is just an expensive department store. I don't really feel like shopping.*

"Wait a minute." Aimee led the way. "Now, look up."

"Wowza!" Leah gulped.

Amanda reluctantly looked up and then gasped. Above her was a stained-glass dome like a huge Tiffany lampshade. She stood mesmerised.

"At Christmas-time they suspend a large decorated Christmas tree from the centre of the dome, sometimes upside down. It is magical." Aimee's brown eyes sparkled. "The store is really old, it opened in 1912."

"This is the most amazing department store I have ever been in!" Leah exclaimed.

"It feels more like a cathedral or a theatre than a store." Amanda counted four floors visible from the middle of the open round hall they were standing in. Glittering gold arches on each floor revealed the latest fashions and accessories.

A commotion at the front door took Amanda's thoughts away from the splendour of the store. "What now?"

Police officers gathered around the front of the store, allowing no one in or out. A young man in a black jacket shook his head and waved his arms, as if arguing with them. After a few minutes, he got on a black Honda scooter and sped away.

Amanda looked at Leah. "That looked like the guy you were talking to at the bookstore this morning."

Leah blushed. "It did look a bit like Jerome."

Aimee glanced at Leah and frowned.

Once the *gendarme* cleared the doorway, Aunt Jenny suggested they return to the bookstore. "I think we've had quite enough excitement for one evening." She sighed and rubbed her brow.

* * *

The next morning Aimee informed them that the bomb scare had proved to be a hoax.

"Real or not, it sure was scary." Amanda cleaned her glasses before putting them on. "Who would do that anyway?"

"Just some stupid people trying to make a point, I guess," said Leah as she pulled her hair back in a ponytail. She stopped midway and stared.

"What is it?"

"Nothing really, just something Jerome said yesterday."

"What? What did he say?"

"Something about in order to make people listen and take notice, you sometimes need to do something drastic."

"What did he mean by that?" Amanda's eyes grew wider.

"We were talking about the French Revolution. I said it was awful how so many people were sent to the guillotine and beheaded, including Queen Marie Antoinette."

"Do you think he was involved in the bomb scare?"

"No, nothing like that. He's just an ordinary guy making small talk."

Amanda had an uneasy feeling. "Let's get downstairs and do our shift in the bookstore."

Leah shrugged. "Whatever."

Fiona, ready to open the store, greeted them when they arrived downstairs. Philippe Lawrence was waiting outside and kissed Fiona on both cheeks when she opened the door. "I wanted to get here early to do some research before the store got busy." He noticed the girls standing behind Fiona and smiled. "I hope you got back all right last night."

6

DURING A LULL IN THE BOOKSTORE, AMANDA LEAFED THROUGH
a book about Joan of Arc.

"Do you like books about famous women?"

She looked up to see Philippe Lawrence standing beside
her. "Yes, I do. I especially like Joan of Arc because she was
so brave. I wish I could be brave like that."

"Oh, I think you are. You managed very well during the
bomb scare."

"No, I didn't. I was only concerned about getting out of
the building. I didn't once think about helping anyone else."

"Well, we have to look after ourselves before we can look
after others. We would be of no use to anyone else if we
were hurt or trapped, would we?"

"I guess." She shrugged. "How is your research coming
along?"

"Quite well, thanks. I want to ask you how well you know
the young man, Jerome."

"Oh, I don't know him at all. He was here the other
day, but he was talking to Leah. Why? Is he in some kind of
trouble?"

"No. At least I don't think so. If you see him around,
could you let me know?" He handed her a business card

with his name and phone number on it.

Aunt Jenny arrived and announced, "It's almost lunchtime. I want to take you girls to my favourite place in Paris." She smiled sweetly at Philippe. "Would you care to join us, Mr. Lawrence?"

"Thank you, that is very kind, but I must be going." He looked at his watch. "I have a previous engagement and I'm running late. Enjoy your lunch."

"He's a bit of a dark horse, isn't he?" said Aunt Jenny when he left the store.

"What does that mean?" asked Amanda.

"A dark horse refers to a person who keeps their interests and abilities a secret. Often they have a talent or skill that comes as a surprise. We know very little about him, but he keeps showing up."

"That's true. He was asking about Jerome, which I thought was strange."

"Really?" Leah stepped out from behind a bookshelf and frowned.

❋ ❋ ❋

Aunt Jenny took them down busy, narrow streets with people rushing along, many carrying a baguette in a brown paper bag under their arm. They often shouted "*Bonjour*" as they passed. Amanda noticed some nibbling on the end of the bread as they made their way. She loved the charming outdoor cafes with folks sipping coffee, reading a paper or murmuring "mmm" as they bit into a tasty pastry.

"Can we have lunch at one of these places?" Amanda asked Aunt Jenny.

"No, not today. I have a place in mind you will love. It's just around the corner."

In a few minutes, she stopped in front of a tall, narrow, cream-coloured building sandwiched between two other buildings. Above the awning, ODETTE was printed in large letters.

Amanda thought it was cute but not that special. Noticing one table with three chairs in front, she headed toward it before anyone else took it.

"No, Amanda, this way." Aunt Jenny motioned as she went inside. Amanda sighed and shrugged. She really wanted to eat outside but followed the others. Aunt Jenny chatted in French with the girl behind the glass counter, then pointed to rows of fancy French pastries as well as baguettes stuffed with cheese and meats. "Decide what you'd like."

Once everyone ordered, the waitress took them up two flights of narrow stairs and led them to a table in front of a shuttered window. She tugged at the wooden shutters until they squeaked open, letting in a flood of sunshine.

Amanda gasped. She closed her eyes for a second and then opened them. In front of her was a picture-perfect view of Notre-Dame Cathedral, the impressive spire poking up from behind a large tree.

"Unbelievable! What a fabulous view." She sucked in a quick breath and swallowed. "Thanks so much for bringing us to this place."

Aunt Jenny pulled out a chair. "I'm glad we could have lunch here. The girl said that the upstairs wasn't open today as they are short-staffed. But I told her you came all the way from Canada and I wanted you to experience this, so she opened it just for us."

Amanda grinned, pleased that they were eating inside with the amazing view.

After devouring the baguettes, a plate of six *choux à la crème* was brought up from downstairs.

Amanda chose one filled with pistachio cream and another with praline cream. "These are so yummy, sort of like cream puffs." She wiped her mouth with the napkin provided.

She took one last look at the stunning cathedral and remembered the feeling of awe she'd had when she was inside it. Looking down onto the street below, Amanda noticed a motor scooter parked in front of an old church. Someone wearing a black jacket crouched behind a flowering bush in a large pot near the church.

"Can we check out that little church on the street in front of Odette's? There might be an interesting graveyard."

Leah rolled her eyes. "You and your strange fascination with graveyards."

Aunt Jenny said, "Of course. I love Église Saint-Julien-le-Pauvre. In English, it means Church of Saint Julian the Poor, and it's the city's oldest religious building. I once attended a performance of the music of Chopin there. Fabulous acoustics."

They descended the narrow stairs of the restaurant and thanked the girl behind the counter. When they got outside and entered the churchyard, the sky had clouded over. Amanda scanned the grounds. There wasn't anyone hiding by the large pot anymore.

"The church is closed, so we can't go inside," said Aunt Jenny. "Sorry, there isn't a cemetery but there is an interesting square behind the church with a very old tree, if I remember correctly."

They walked around the old stone building to Square Rene Viviani, where an old tree stood propped up by a concrete post. A sign in front explained that it was a locust tree, the oldest tree in Paris, and had been planted in 1602 by the gardener-in-chief who had served three different French kings.

"Look at that," exclaimed Amanda. "It says here it is the Lucky Tree of Paris and it can bring years of good luck to those who gently touch the tree's bark."

"I don't think that guy touched it." Leah pointed to a young man being taken away by two uniformed police officers. It was too far away for Amanda to see his face, but he was wearing a black jacket.

7

"WOULD YOU LIKE TO GO TO THE LOUVRE THIS AFTERNOON?" asked Aunt Jenny.

Amanda's eyes lit up. "Isn't that where the Mona Lisa is?"

"Yes, but there's always so many stupid people crowding around it," answered Leah.

"Have you seen it?"

"When I was eight years old I saw it with my mum. I remember it was very crowded. She took her eyes off me and I guess I wandered away. She was totally frantic when she found me. I got treated to ice cream, as she thought it was all her fault. She still apologizes when she talks about it." Leah chuckled.

"You had better both stick with me this time." Aunt Jenny led them across another bridge. "The Louvre was originally a Royal Palace, the home of the French kings, until Louis XIV moved his household to Versailles. Since then it's been used to house works of art. It's the largest and most visited museum in the world. Fortunately, I have an app on my phone where I can get tickets so we don't have to wait in line. It also shows me where all the displays are so we don't waste time looking for things."

They stopped in front of a massive old building. Amanda remarked, "This does look like a palace. Everything in Paris is so—so grand!" She noticed displays of white sculptures through large windows as they went through a stone passageway. "Will we be seeing those?"

"Of course. The Venus de Milo is here as well. You'll want to see that."

They entered a large open courtyard. "The main entrance is over there." Aunt Jenny pointed to an enormous glass pyramid. It looked quite modern surrounded by the old stone buildings and walls.

"That is so cool."

"It's a fairly new addition, built in 1989. Some people weren't in favour of it at first, but I like it. It adds to the environment." Aunt Jenny opened her purse and took out her phone. "And because you are both under eighteen, you can get in free."

Amanda loved the museum and was awestruck when she saw the armless ancient Greek statue of Venus de Milo. She had seen pictures on the internet, but there was nothing like seeing it in person. She couldn't wait to tell her teacher all about it.

While waiting to see the famous Mona Lisa, they noticed many people taking pictures of themselves near the tiny painting with selfie sticks. It was very crowded, and everyone wanted a turn. Amanda felt uncomfortable and shifted from foot to foot.

She looked around. "I need to find a bathroom."

"I saw a sign for one just back there." Leah pointed. "You have time, we aren't anywhere near the painting yet."

On the way back from the bathroom, the lights went out. Amanda froze. Someone brushed by her. *Oh no, not another bomb scare. Or maybe someone is trying to steal a painting, maybe even the Mona Lisa.*

Suddenly the lights came back on. Amanda heard shouting. She rushed toward the noise to see what was going on. Near the Mona Lisa two men scuffled. One accused the other of bumping him with his selfie stick. He had the man by the collar, trying to take the stick away from him. The other man flailed around, holding onto his selfie stick with one hand while attempting to hit the accuser with the other. He stepped backward to avoid a punch and stumbled into Amanda. No one noticed her fall to the floor.

When she opened her eyes, she was on her back in a sea of legs. She rolled over, got up on her hands and knees and crawled out just as security guards arrived to separate the two angry men.

"Here, let me help you up."

A hand reached down to her. She looked up into the brown eyes of Philippe Lawrence as he helped her to her feet.

Aunt Jenny and Leah rushed over to her. "Amanda, what were you doing on the floor?"

She pointed to the men being ushered away by security guards. "One of those guys knocked me over."

"They should ban selfie sticks." Philippe looked at the

men in disgust. He turned back to Amanda. "Are you all right?"

She brushed dust off her jeans. "Yes, thanks."

"Let's get out of here," said Leah. "It's too crowded."

"I agree," said Amanda. "I got a glimpse of Mona Lisa and her almost smile." Amanda pressed her lips together and tried to smile like the woman in the painting, which made Leah laugh.

"This way would be best," said Philippe and led them outside.

They left the building and entered the courtyard. A young woman in a long black coat played a violin near a marble column. Amanda took a picture and dropped a euro into her open case.

Aunt Jenny and Philippe, deep in conversation, found a bench to sit on.

Amanda stood on a square pillar and pointed at the tip of the glass pyramid while Leah took her picture. "I wonder why the lights went out?" she asked.

"It was probably just a power cut. It wasn't for long," replied Leah.

"It felt long for me," said Amanda. "Now I know how you must have felt when you got separated from your mom."

Leah nodded. "I think she was more upset than I was."

＊ ＊ ＊

They all made their way back across the river just as the setting sun cast an odd glow.

As they neared the bookstore, Aimee rushed up to them out of breath. "Have you heard?" She turned to point. "The cathedral is on fire!"

"No! Not Notre-Dame?" Amanda covered her mouth with her hand.

"Yes, Our Lady." Aimee had tears in her eyes. "They are trying to save the many precious artifacts. I'm going to help. Philippe, you must come too."

Philippe paled and shook his head slowly. "I thought something like this might happen," he mumbled as he picked up the pace.

Amanda, Leah, and Aunt Jenny followed in silence.

In the distance, ominous smoke billowed up into the sky.

8

THE SCENT OF CENTURIES-OLD WOOD AND ANCIENT BOOKS burning caught in Amanda's throat. She took off her glasses and rubbed her stinging eyes. How could this amazing building be on fire?

Smoke rose from Notre-Dame as pigeons circled above.

Approaching the cathedral, Amanda was relieved to see that the two front columns were not ablaze. Behind the towers, though, the roof erupted in flames. People scurried past. Crowds formed. A multitude of phones and cameras recorded history burning. Sirens wailed from police cars. Fire trucks sped by. She heard a man shout, *"Allez les pompiers!"* Another joined in, "Yes, let's go, firefighters!"

She coughed and the smoke made her eyes water. Swiping away a tear rolling down her cheek, she noticed black soot on her finger. She glanced at Leah. Black specks clung to her hair and face. Leah pulled out the phone from her back pocket, took a couple of pictures, shook her head, and put it back.

Police blew whistles, keeping onlookers back. Firefighters carrying huge hoses sprayed the building. Water flowed down the stones like a waterfall. Gargoyles appeared to be crying while liquid spouted from their mouths.

Amanda felt the intense heat coming off the stones. She

followed Philippe and Aimee around to a side door where a line of people were forming. She watched as firefighters and police officers handed items out from the church to the first person, who handed it to the next, forming a human chain.

"Can we help?" asked Amanda, eager to do whatever she could.

An exhausted police officer approached the group, shaking his head and waving his hands. "No children allowed."

Philippe said something in French.

"OK, Monsieur Lawrence. *C'est bon.*" The officer shrugged his shoulders and carried on.

"I told him you were all with me and I'd make sure you would stay out of danger. We should be fine here at the end of the line, away from potential falling debris."

Aunt Jenny, Aimee, Leah, Amanda, and Philippe became part of the human chain. While the fire raged on, precious relics were removed from the cathedral and taken away to safety. Proud to be part of the rescue, Amanda carefully passed old books, boxes of artifacts, paintings, and tapestries on to the next person in the chain.

As night fell and the sky grew darker, roaring flames rose higher, painting the sky bright red, orange, and yellow. From inside, the sounds of crackling and falling timbers caused Amanda to shiver when she thought of the destruction. As if at a funeral, the crowd watched silently.

Suddenly there was a collective gasp. Amanda gazed up. The spire looked like a red hot poker against the black sky. It bent forward and toppled into the nave. Sparks flew.

White hot flames shot up in the air. It was gone.

Amanda heard sobbing behind her. An older lady put her hand over her mouth and turned from the sight. Her husband put his arm around her shaking shoulders and led her away. An immense sadness crushed Amanda's chest. Her glasses fogged up as her eyes prickled with tears.

One lonely voice started to sing and then another. Soon everyone joined in singing "Ave Maria" softly in French, dedicated to the love of their church. A lump formed in her throat as Amanda remembered being inside and listening to the choir just two days before.

A firefighter came out of the church and made an announcement.

"We have to go," said Philippe. "That is all we can save as it is getting too dangerous to be inside collecting items. Thankfully, most of the important things have been saved."

"We should go back to the bookstore," said Aunt Jenny.

"That's a good idea." Philippe placed his hand on Aunt Jenny's shoulder. He suddenly looked much older. "Thanks for helping."

Amanda felt a heaviness in her legs as they walked back through the throngs crowding the bridges, riverbanks, and streets. They passed television crews set up and reporting from the banks of the Seine. Boats dotted the river, carrying observers. Police vessels circled the Île de la Cité.

This was an evening she would never forget.

* * *

"What a night! I wonder how the fire started." Leah slumped onto her bed. "I sure hope it wasn't done on purpose."

Amanda's hands hung at her sides. "That beautiful building, destroyed." She choked back a tear.

Aunt Jenny looked up from her phone. "I've just been on my Twitter feed and it's thought the fire started in the wooden roof. They've been doing some restoration work there recently. Those oak timbers were very old, from the twelfth century. You know the roof was often called 'the forest' because it was made of many beams of oak, each from a different tree." She sighed. "Now all gone."

"I'm going to have a bath." Amanda ran her hands through her hair. "My clothes, hair, and everything smells of smoke."

"I'll be next if I don't fall asleep." Leah leaned back on her pillow and dug out her phone. "This was just the worst. I'm going to send the pictures to Mum and Dad."

The warm water felt good as Amanda soaked in the big cast-iron tub, her mind full of images of the burning cathedral. She wished she hadn't been in Paris when it happened. She wished it hadn't happened at all. She wished she was back home in Canada with her parents.

I'm not going to let this ruin my trip to this amazing city.

Amanda thought about what had happened so far. *Was the fire in Notre-Dame connected to the bomb scare at the Opera House? Or the lights going out at the Louvre? Did Philippe Lawrence have anything to do with these events? He was always there! And everyone seemed to know him.*

9

AMANDA FELT LIKE SHE HADN'T SLEPT AT ALL, EVEN THOUGH she had been exhausted when she fell into bed. She heard Aimee come in late.

That morning everyone in the bookshop was subdued, even the shoppers.

"Is there any news about how the fire started?" asked Amanda as she dusted bookshelves.

"No, it may have been the workers, but they are not sure," replied Aimee, rearranging books in the history section. "Here is a book about Notre-Dame you might find interesting." She handed it to Amanda.

"Thanks. That's great. I think I'll do a report on the cathedral for my teacher in Canada." Amanda leafed through the book, then looked up. "Do you know much about Mr. Lawrence?"

Aimee concentrated on organizing books. "Not much. I met him here while he was doing research on a book he's writing. Why do you ask?"

"I don't know. It just seems strange that he's always around when there's a problem, and also everyone seems to know him."

"Umm." Aimee bit her bottom lip. "He is very popular

42

and has lived in Paris off and on for many years."

"Where else does he live?"

"In England."

"Is he English or French?"

"Both. His mother is French and his father is English."

"I guess that's why he can speak both languages so well. I wish I could do that."

"Isn't Canada a bilingual country?"

"It is. We learn French in school, but we don't get to practice it much unless we live in the province of Quebec. I'm from Alberta, and not many people speak French there."

Just then Aunt Jenny joined them and asked if they had seen Leah.

"No, I haven't." Amanda shook her head. "I thought she was with you."

"I was thinking of taking you girls to the Palace of Versailles today. It will be good to get out of the city. Can you see if you can find her? We need to catch a bus soon."

Amanda looked in the bedroom and the kitchen, but there was no sign of her friend. She checked outside, but Leah was not there or in the coffee shop either. A flash of white caught her eye as the bookstore cat, Aggie, dashed around the corner. Amanda followed her to the back of the building, where she heard voices. She stopped short when she saw Leah chatting to a guy leaning against a motor scooter, his back to her.

"Were you there last night?" asked Leah.

"I was across town. I saw the fire from on top of Montmartre. It looked pretty bad." The guy shrugged his shoulders. "You don't think I had anything to do with it, do you?"

"You better not have." Leah scowled.

Amanda cleared her throat. Jerome turned, saw her, and reddened. Leah opened her mouth.

"Aunt Jenny's looking for you. We're going to Versailles in a few minutes."

"I have to go anyway. Don't let that Lawrence fellow know you saw me." Jerome pushed his scooter out into the alley behind the store, climbed on it, and sped away.

"What was he doing here?" asked Amanda.

Leah shrugged. "I don't know. Seems he's hiding from someone. What do we know about Philippe Lawrence?"

"Not much." Amanda realized she hadn't got a lot of info about Philippe from Aimee.

* * *

The bus ride to Versailles, a town on the outskirts of Paris, only took thirty minutes. Amanda was excited because she had read all about the palace King Louis XIV built from what used to be his father's hunting lodge. But she wasn't at all prepared for its grandeur.

The building glistened in the sun as the bus pulled into the parking lot. In front stood a majestic statue of the Sun King, Louis XIV, on a horse. The huge entrance gate, covered in gold and topped with a golden crown on top of a large smiling sun, opened into an immense cobblestone courtyard.

"Now I can see why they called him the Sun King," remarked Amanda as she looked up at the grey slate roof trimmed in gold filigree and more smiling gold suns. Even the balconies and window frames were trimmed in gold.

"He reigned France for seventy-two years, the longest reigning European monarch," explained Aunt Jenny.

They joined a long line of tourists waiting to get inside the palace. Aunt Jenny had booked tickets online beforehand, so it didn't take them long to enter. Once inside, Amanda's jaw dropped. She had never seen anything so opulent. Floors of inlaid marble, walls and ceilings covered in art, statues in every corner, and gold sprinkled everywhere. Room after room seemed fancier than the last one.

They passed through a small chamber with red-flocked wallpaper trimmed in gold. A bed with a brocade bedspread, canopy, and red velvet curtains took up most of the room. A gold headboard featured yet another golden sun. A sign indicated it was the king's bedchamber.

"Pretty fancy." Amanda took a picture.

"If you think this is fancy, wait until you see the Hall of Mirrors." Aunt Jenny pointed the way.

They entered a long hallway glittering with crystal chandeliers. On one side, floor-to-ceiling mirrors reflected tourists walking by, paintings, and sculptures. Amanda took a picture of herself taking a picture of a mirror.

On the other side, Amanda peered out the windows that looked over the gardens. "Will you look at this?"

Leah came over to see. "Seriously! They have to be the

best gardens anywhere." She squinted and pointed. "Is that Jerome by the cone-shaped tree down there?"

Amanda adjusted her glasses. "It's too far away to tell."

Leah rolled her eyes. "Honestly. He knew we were coming here." She shouted to Aunt Jenny who was taking a picture of a marble sculpture at the other end of the room. "Can we go look around the gardens?"

"Go ahead. I'm going to make some notes. Take your time. Meet me back at the coffee shop." Aunt Jenny headed for a cup of tea while Amanda and Leah hurried to the gardens.

10

METICULOUSLY MANICURED TREES AND SHRUBS SURROUNDED sparkling fountains and lined pathways in the immense garden that stretched far into the distance. Marble sculptures stood among the trees like silent observers.

"This is unreal. Like stepping into Alice's wonderland! Imagine how many people it must take to keep this so—so perfect." Amanda pulled out her camera.

"No time to sightsee and take pictures, Amanda. We need to see if that was Jerome and find out what he's up to. If he is following us, I want to know why." Leah picked up the pace.

Amanda bit her bottom lip and put her camera away. *What has got into Leah?*

They circled a massive tiered fountain with water spraying up from the middle onto a statue of a woman and two children perched on top. Gold frogs lounged on the tiers while golden turtles spouted water. Amanda wanted to have a better look, but Leah was walking too fast, oblivious of the splendour around them.

"There! Over there by that fountain. I think someone's lurking behind those trees." Leah pointed. "You go around that way and I'll go this way. Then he'll have nowhere to go."

Yikes! Leah was sounding like an army sergeant or a football coach. Amanda decided to do what she was told.

Sure enough, Jerome was there. He saw Amanda and turned to run in the opposite direction. Leah blocked his way.

"What are you doing, Jerome?" Leah placed her hands firmly on his shoulders.

"I, ummm." Jerome looked across Leah's shoulders. "Please don't shout. I can explain but not here and not now. I mustn't be seen."

Leah raised her eyebrows. "By who?"

Amanda whispered, "Maybe by those guys over there by the fountain?"

Three young men searched in the bushes as they approached the clump of trees.

"Let's get out of here." Jerome led the way down a small path to an enclosed grove with a cascading waterfall at one end.

"Why are we running from those guys? What do they want with you?" demanded Leah.

"They're from a gang that I accidentally joined. I don't want to belong anymore, but they won't let me leave."

"How can you accidentally join a gang?"

"Not now! It's a long story."

"I'll just tell them to leave you alone," said Amanda.

"No way! They have knives." Jerome put up his hands to stop her. "Look, this place is a labyrinth of paths and groves. If we go this way, we can lose them."

Running down the path, in and out of small gardens and around more elaborate fountains, Amanda kept looking behind her. The gang members weren't in sight.

At the bottom of the gardens, golden stallions driven by a man on a chariot emerged from the waters of the biggest fountain yet.

"OK, they're gone." Jerome stopped to catch his breath and look around. There was no one else nearby.

"This is the most amazing fountain I have ever seen." Amanda really wanted to take a picture but didn't dare annoy Leah.

"This is the fountain of Apollo, the sun god," Jerome replied. "It is pretty good. But think of the money that was spent on it, while the peasants starved. This whole place is an example of how the aristocracy lived in grandeur while the rest of the citizens struggled to put food in their mouths. It's no wonder the people eventually revolted." He sucked in a deep breath.

Leah looked at her watch. "We should get back to Aunt Jenny."

"You go ahead. I'm just going to take a couple of pictures." Amanda pulled out her camera and aimed it at the sculpture in the fountain. Leah and Jerome started walking up the path.

Caught up in taking pictures, Amanda didn't notice a young man approach until he was right beside her.

"Where is your friend Jerome? We need to speak with him."

Amanda felt the hair lift on the nape of her neck. She slowly lowered her camera and turned around. "I don't know. Besides, he is not my friend."

"He's a friend of the blond girl and he was here with you not long ago." The teenager sneered, glaring at her with unfriendly eyes.

Amanda shook her head. Her lips trembled. "I—I don't think so."

The fellow reached his dragon-tattooed arm down toward his foot. She remembered what Jerome had said about knives and slowly backed away, toward the fountain. The guy lunged forward. She thought she saw a flash of metal in his hand and shrieked. Ducking out of the way, she noticed the tiles were wet. The guy slipped, tried to catch himself, but fell headfirst into the fountain.

As she raced up the path, toward the palace, Amanda heard him splashing around and swearing in French. Heart beating fast, she wondered where the other two gang members were.

She was near the palace when she spotted them ahead on the path she needed to take. To get to the coffee shop she would have to pass them. Before they saw her, Amanda ducked into an opening which led to an enclosed courtyard. Not sure where to go, she entered an arched doorway leading down a long hallway with black and white tiles on the floor. Lined with standing white figurines, it opened up to a large room. Huge paintings depicting war scenes covered the walls. She stopped in front of one of a young girl in full armour mounted on a horse with soldiers surrounding her and people cheering her on.

"Jeanne d'Arc. That is your hero if I remember correctly."

Amanda's heart stopped. She turned around and found herself face-to-face with Philippe Lawrence.

II

AMANDA CROSSED HER ARMS. "WHAT ARE YOU DOING HERE?"

"I could ask you the same thing. You always seem to be where I am." Philippe smirked, then he cleared his throat. "Did you happen to see three or four young men, teenagers actually, looking a bit tough? You know, leather jackets, tattoos, body piercings. They ride motor scooters. One of them is an English kid called Jerome."

"Lots of guys look like that. Why?"

"I need to talk to them, that's all."

Amanda shoved her hands into her pockets. "I thought you were a writer."

"I am. They could give me some information for the book I'm writing, a book about gangs."

"So, you're doing research?"

"Yes. That's what I'm doing—research." He scratched his head. "Where are Leah and Jenny—I mean Ms. Anderson?"

"In the coffee shop. I'm supposed to meet them there. I just wanted to see this painting."

"How about I walk with you? I need a coffee, even though it will be expensive here."

Amanda nodded. "Yeah, sure. That would be good." She

really didn't believe him, but it was probably a good idea to be with someone if she encountered the gang members again.

They climbed an elaborate marble staircase that took them to the coffee shop.

Leah waved. "We're over here. Aunt Jenny bought some macarons to have with our tea. Oh, I see you brought Mr. Lawrence with you."

"Can I buy you ladies some more tea?" asked Philippe.

"That would be nice. The pot of tea I ordered is now cold." Aunt Jenny smiled. "I'll come with you." She followed Philippe to the counter.

"What took you so long?" Leah hissed.

"Later." Amanda lowered her voice. "Where's Jerome? Mr. Lawrence is looking for him. And the others."

"He left on his scooter." Leah glanced over at Philippe. "You didn't tell him Jerome was here, did you?"

"No." Amanda reached for a lime-green macaron. "I just don't know who to believe right now."

Philippe and Aunt Jenny returned with a tray of tea.

"So, can you tell us more about the book you're writing?" Amanda asked Philippe.

"Well, it's crime mystery. About a gang of young boys who get caught up in terrorist activities. They don't realize what they've got themselves into until it's too late. Bad things happen, people get killed, and the police have to solve the mystery before more people get hurt. It all happens in the 1960s."

"You mean there were terrorists then too?" Leah asked.

"Terrorists have been around for a very long time, I'm afraid. In fact, part of the French Revolution between 1787 and 1799 was called the Reign of Terror. Before that, while Louis XIV was building this very palace, he was constantly worried about people trying to sabotage his construction projects. The king employed secret police to keep an eye on things. They had some horrifying ways of punishing those who they suspected, like the hanging cages."

"What's a hanging cage?"

"It's like a large bird cage hung in alcoves around the castle. People suspected of acts of terrorism or sabotage were left to hang in them without food and water as an example to anyone who might think of doing something similar."

Amanda shuddered. Her great-aunt Mary would say someone had walked over her grave.

"Have you girls seen enough?" asked Aunt Jenny. "I'd like to get back to the bookstore and type up my notes."

"Sure, I'm good," said Leah.

"Me too. Thanks for bringing me here. I love this place. Just glad we didn't see any hanging cages." Amanda popped the last crunchy macaron into her mouth and drained her cup of tea.

"I need to get going too. I promised to meet someone." Philippe Lawrence placed his fedora on his head and tied a bright red scarf around his neck. "Let me know if you have any information for me, Amanda."

Leah glanced at Amanda with a questioning look.

* * *

They returned to Shakespeare and Company just as Fiona was leaving.

"I'm glad you're back. We are a bit short-staffed, so could one of you spend some time in the bookstore? I have to go out for an hour or so. I thought Aimee would be volunteering today, but I haven't seen her."

Amanda raised her hand. "I can help out."

"Sorry, but I have stuff to do," mumbled Leah.

"Like what?" Amanda asked.

"Just—stuff." Leah shrugged. "Be right back."

Aunt Jenny frowned as Leah left through the back door. "I'll quickly type up my notes from this morning and then help out too."

Amanda was pointing out the science fiction section to a young couple when Leah came rushing into the store. She saw Amanda and mouthed, "I need to tell you something."

Amanda excused herself and turned to her distraught friend. "What is it?"

"I just saw your buddy, Philippe Lawrence, in a serious discussion with Aimee. They were studying maps and papers. I think they're planning something. Maybe something dangerous."

12

AMANDA NARROWED HER EYES. "WHAT DO YOU MEAN? HOW do you know it's something dangerous?"

Leah picked at her manicured fingernails. "They kept looking around and covering the notes and maps with their hands."

"That could mean anything, Leah. This isn't like you to be so suspicious. Isn't that my job?" Amanda raised her eyebrows.

Leah lowered her voice. "When Philippe dropped his pen and leaned down to pick it up, I'm sure I saw a gun inside his jacket." She trembled. "I just don't trust him."

The front door opened and Fiona rushed in. "Is everything OK?"

"Yes, all good. It wasn't very busy," answered Amanda.

"It's quiet out there on the streets too. Everyone is so sad about the cathedral."

"Do they know who started the fire?" asked Leah. "Was it terrorists?"

"They still don't know and are investigating. Thankfully the statues of the apostles had been taken away for restoration a few days before, and most of the precious artifacts were saved by the human chain."

"What will happen to the cathedral now?" asked Amanda.

"The president announced they will start the repair of the cathedral immediately. The good news is many wealthy people have come forward with large donations toward the cost of repairs."

A young couple approached the counter, ready to pay for their purchase. Fiona went to help them.

Aunt Jenny arrived and told the girls she would take over at the store so they could go for lunch.

"So, what did you have to do that was so important?" demanded Amanda once they were out of the store.

"I just wanted to be sure Jerome got back and was all right." Leah looked around.

"Well, did he?"

"I don't know, I didn't see him. When I saw Aimee with Philippe, I left because I didn't want them to see me."

"I didn't think they knew each other that well." Amanda scratched her head. "This is weird. Perhaps they're working on a novel together."

"I just don't buy that. And why would he be carrying a gun?" questioned Leah.

"Perhaps you watch too many movies."

"I don't need to watch movies. This terrorism stuff is real. A terrorist drove into pedestrians on Westminster Bridge in London and killed three of them. Many others were injured. It's scary out there these days." Leah flinched.

A young man in a musketeer costume stood in front of them. "It is the *mademoiselle* from Canada and her friend, *non*?" He plucked off his feathered tricorn hat and swept it in front of them as he bowed.

Amanda giggled. "You are so theatrical, Pierre."

"Let me introduce you to my fellow Musketeers, Athos and Aramis, at your service." Two young men with him removed their hats and also bowed with a flourish.

"We just finished a dress rehearsal and we are starving," said the one he called Athos.

"I love that book, *The Three Musketeers*, by Alexandre Dumas." Amanda turned to Pierre. "Then you must be Porthos."

"*Oui. C'est moi.* Yes, I am. We are about to have lunch. Will you join us?"

"Sure, where would you suggest?"

"My house, of course. *Ma maman* is the best cook in town and is expecting us."

"Are you sure she won't mind?"

"But of course not. She loves to cook for my friends and always makes more than we can eat. Come this way."

Leah texted her aunt to let her know where they would be having lunch, while Pierre led them down the street.

"Watch for the *crotte de chien*!" shouted Pierre.

"What?" Amanda looked down just as she was about to step on a dog turd. "Yuck. Don't they pick up after their dogs here?"

"Not very often, even though there is a big fine." Pierre grinned.

They soon arrived at an apartment block with a massive

front door. Once inside, they took a rickety elevator, which looked like a cage, to the sixth floor. As soon as he opened the door to the apartment, delicious smells of onions, butter, and apple pie welcomed them.

"*Maman*, I am home and I have brought some friends."

A large woman, wearing a long apron over a black dress, greeted them with a huge smile. Pierre introduced Amanda and Leah to his mother, Yvette Duchamp, who immediately smothered them in hugs and kisses. She smelled of fresh baked bread.

"*S'il vous plaît*, please, come sit down. I have made a salad with goat cheese, onion soup, and fresh baguette with a *tarte tatin* in the oven for dessert."

Amanda cut through the crunchy cheese covered crouton with her spoon and scooped up a spoonful of onion soup. It was like a taste explosion inside her mouth.

"Yum, this is so good."

Soon the conversation turned to the fire in the cathedral.

"The cathedral is 850 years old and has withstood many wars and even a revolution, only to be destroyed by a fire." Pierre's mother shook her head. "It is so sad."

"But, I wonder who could have started it?" asked Amanda.

"They don't know yet," replied Pierre. "They have a top-notch team investigating."

"*Merci*, the stained-glass windows and the church organ appear to be undamaged," said Madame Duchamp as she stacked the empty bowls. "They have transferred the sacred artwork and artifacts that were saved to the Louvre

Museum." She sighed. "You know there have been a spate of attacks on the churches in France recently."

"That's true. There's been a rising hostility in France against the church and its symbols," said one of the young men. "Radicals say that it poisons the minds of the citizens."

Madame Duchamp shuddered. "I don't like that kind of talk. Remember how bad things got the last time there was a revolution. We should all be free to worship, or not, as we choose. But to try to destroy a part of history, a work of art—that is a crime." She swiped away a tear and took the bowls into the kitchen.

"Maman gets very emotional about all of this. She is an artist, a sculptor. Her work is shown in art galleries all over the world. Nothing is more precious to her than history and art," explained Pierre.

"Do you think it might have been terrorists that started the fire?" asked Leah.

"Perhaps," said the boy playing Aramis. "I have heard talk it could be the work of gangs. There has been trouble again between some kids on motor scooters and the police. These gangs are terrible. They trick boys into joining them, then make them do illegal things."

"What? How can they trick them into joining?" Amanda's eyes widened.

Pierre put his finger to his lips as his mother returned with a steaming dessert straight from the oven. She sliced through the crisp pastry top, revealing a filling of caramelized apples, and placed a spoonful on each plate. Then she added a dollop of *crème fraîche*.

Amanda blew on it and took a mouthful. She grinned. "What did you say this was called?"

"It is a *tarte tatin*. It is like an upside-down apple pie with the crust on the top. It was accidentally invented by the Tatin sisters who ran a hotel in the 1880s."

"It is so delicious. Can I have the recipe? I would love to make it for my mom and dad."

"But of course. I will email it to you."

13

"I UNDERSTAND YOU'RE A POTTER, MRS. DUCHAMP. WHERE IS your studio?"

Pierre's mother pointed up. "It is here in the attic. Would you like to see it?"

Amanda beamed. "I would love that. Thanks, Mrs.—I mean *Madame* Du . . . "

"*S'il vous plait*, please, call me Yvette. All of Pierre's friends do."

Leah looked at her watch. "Amanda, we should go. Aunt Jenny will wonder where we are."

"*Oui*. The Musketeers need to get back to the theatre and practice sword fighting." Pierre picked up his hat and opened the door.

"Come back and visit again and I will show you my studio. Have you been to Monet's garden yet? If you like his paintings, you will see how he was inspired. Also, you should go the Musée d'Orsay. It is even better than the Louvre, in my opinion."

"Thank you for the delicious meal." Amanda gave Yvette a big hug. "It was so great to meet you."

* * *

The next morning Amanda asked Aunt Jenny if they could visit Monet's garden.

"But of course. I was planning to go there, and we really should get out of the city. The air still smells of smoke, everyone is down, and there is so much speculation about who or what started the fire in the cathedral."

They asked Fiona if they could do their shifts in the bookstore later that afternoon.

"No problem." Fiona handed Amanda a book about the painter Claude Monet. "You will enjoy this."

Amanda looked through the book on the bus. They drove past the lush green French countryside dotted with white cows and lavender fields, to the village of Giverny where the painter produced many of his famous paintings. Her mom had taken her to a Monet exhibition in Calgary, and she couldn't wait to see the gardens that inspired his art.

✻ ✻ ✻

"Unbelievable! Where do we start?" Amanda gawked at a sea of cheerful flowers and pulled out her camera.

Narrow gravel paths took them through rows of red and yellow poppies, purple and white irises, and bushes covered in pompoms of primary colours. She moved carefully as she crept closer to take pictures of the plants. Amanda felt like she had stepped into a painting . . . a Monet painting.

They walked around a small lake surrounded by weeping willows and filled with delicate water lilies. At the end of the lake, a curved green bridge dripped with overhanging purple wisteria.

"My mom has a print of this in her office. Wait till she sees I've actually been here!" Amanda snapped more pictures.

Leah gave her a slight push. "Go stand on the bridge and I'll take your picture."

Amanda found a spot under the wisteria on the crowded bridge and smiled for Leah. Two women chatted loudly in English behind her. One said, "And they saw some boys on motor scooters ride away from the church. I bet they started the fire."

"That's awful. They should be put away for life. Young people have no respect. No respect at all," the other replied.

Amanda shivered.

They found Aunt Jenny on her phone, sitting on a bench outside a pink house with bright green shutters: the house Claude Monet and his family had lived in. She nodded and waved at them.

Leah pointed to the green front door. "We're going inside."

The cosy house, filled with the famous painter's work and that of his artist friends, felt like a happy place. His studio overlooked the gardens. Amanda envisioned him sitting at his desk, sketching scenes while the children played in the garden.

"Did you see her?"

Leah took her out of her reverie.

Amanda gave her head a shake. "Who?"

"The girl with corn braids. I'm sure it was Aimee looking out the window at the garden."

"Really? I wonder why she's here. I thought she was working at the bookstore." Amanda glanced around and spotted someone who looked a lot like Aimee going into a bedroom.

"I don't know, but I don't want her to see me," said Leah with a scowl. "I don't know if she saw me the other day, and I just don't trust her."

"Let's see what she's up to," said Amanda.

The girls followed Aimee through the crowded house, hiding behind doors and overstuffed chairs, trying not to be seen. They ran down the stairs and into a large room with copper cooking pots hanging on the walls. No one else was in the bright yellow kitchen. Hearing footsteps, Leah grabbed Amanda's hand and pulled her under the massive farmhouse-style table. They recognized Aimee's high-heeled boots as she circled the table. Amanda gasped when the tablecloth lifted and Aimee peered under.

"What are you two doing under here? Are you hiding from me?"

The girls crept out from their hiding place. "What are you doing here?" asked Amanda.

Aimee laughed. "I'm doing research for my paper on Impressionist painters. I love this place. What do you think of it?"

"Umm, yes, it's awesome." Amanda fidgeted. "Sorry, we—we thought you were someone else."

"That's all right." Aimee grinned. "I meant to tell you that Fiona at the bookstore is really impressed with how you help the customers. I bet you could get a job there when you're old enough."

Amanda blushed.

Aimee turned to Leah. "Leah, you've made some acquaintances too. I think you know a young man called Jerome?"

Leah hesitated. "Well, I may have chatted with him a couple of times."

"Has he mentioned anything about his friends?"

"No, he hasn't mentioned them." Leah looked away.

Aimee wrinkled her brow and looked at her watch. "I best be going. Amanda, there are some good books about Monet and his paintings in the bookstore. I know you're writing a report for your teacher, you might want to check them out. See you both later."

Leah frowned as Aimee left the building. "Why does she want to know about Jerome and his friends? I don't trust her."

Amanda gave a heavy sigh. "I just don't know . . . "

Aunt Jenny walked into the kitchen, waving her hands. "Isn't this place incredible? So peaceful and inspiring. I feel like painting a picture."

14

AUNT JENNY'S CELL PHONE RANG AGAIN. "I'M SO SORRY. IT'S this research I'm doing. It's getting to be more complicated than I thought. Please excuse me, I have to get this. You two explore some more. I'll be right here." She answered the call.

Leah grabbed Amanda's hand. "Let's look around the village. I saw a hat I'd like to check out in one of the shops."

The girls strolled down a narrow street, past lush green hedges, rustic stone walls, and charming old cottages that looked like they should be on a cookie tin. Amanda loved the painted shutters on the windows and the cute letter-boxes beside each door.

"It would be fun to live in a place like this, wouldn't it?" asked Amanda.

Leah shrugged. "It's pretty and quaint but too quiet for me." Her face lit up as she pointed. "There's the shop I saw when we arrived."

Umbrellas, mugs, and T-shirts decorated with Monet's lily pads adorned the front of the shop.

Leah faced a floppy straw hat perched on a mannequin head. "May I try this one?" she asked the shopkeeper.

"*Oui*. But of course." The woman removed the hat from

the mannequin, gently placed it on Leah's head, and directed her to a mirror. "It looks fine on you, *non*?"

Leah grinned from ear to ear. "It looks smashing!"

"You rock that hat! You look like a movie star," said Amanda.

"I really do think I must have it." Leah took out her wallet, pulled out some euros, and paid the clerk.

"Would you like me to put it in a bag, *mademoiselle*?"

"No thank you, I'll wear it."

"*Oui*. But I must remove the tag."

Amanda bought a notebook for her mom and a fridge magnet for her great-aunt Mary.

Happy with their purchases, the girls made their way back to the gardens. Amanda was taking pictures of the houses when a little black dog ran out from behind a bush. It ran straight up to Amanda and wagged its tail non-stop.

"Do you know this dog?" asked Leah.

"I'm not sure." Amanda patted the poodle's head. "She looks a lot like Philippe's dog, Fifi."

"How do you know he has a dog?"

"I saw him walking Fifi in the park at Place des Vosges."

The little dog ran toward a house and then back to Amanda. "What do you want? Are you trying to tell me something?" She looked at Leah. "I think we should follow her."

Leah slowly shook her head. "I don't think that's a good idea."

Amanda paid no attention to her friend and followed the

poodle to a stone cottage with blue shutters on the windows and ivy growing up the side. Leah reluctantly followed. As the girls got nearer they heard a faint moaning sound.

"Someone might be hurt. We need to see if they need help." Amanda tried the door. It wouldn't budge. "I wonder how we can get in."

The poodle jumped like an uncoiled spring and ran around in circles, all the while barking little squeaks. Amanda felt around the doorway. One brick wobbled. She grabbed on it and tugged. The brick popped out, revealing a key with a tag. Amanda took it out and read, "*Boîte aux lettres*, what's that in English?"

Leah checked her phone. "It means letterbox, according to Google Translate."

Amanda tried the key in the red letterbox beside the door. To her surprise, it opened. Inside was another key.

"Honestly! This one better open the door." Leah grabbed the key and inserted it into the lock on the door. The key didn't fit. "Let's just forget it and go back to the gardens."

The dog was going crazy, jumping around. The faint moaning continued.

"Wait," said Amanda, cupping her ear. "I think the sound might be coming from behind the house."

They crept around to the back. No one was there. The dog ran to a low rectangular door and pawed the ground in front of it. Amanda tried the key in the lock, and the door swung open to reveal steps leading down into a cellar. The pup scampered down the stairs into the darkness. The muffled moaning became a bit louder.

Amanda's eyes grew large. "Someone is down there and probably hurt." She moved toward the steps.

Leah pulled her back. "Are you daft? You cannot be thinking of going into that dark cellar. I've seen enough scary movies to know that is not a good idea."

"We have a light on our phones, so it won't be totally dark." Amanda turned on her light and aimed it at the stairs. "Come on."

Leah hesitated, then followed as they crept down into the darkness together. Once at the bottom, Amanda shone her light around. Shelves lined the musty cellar, some piled high with dusty boxes and suitcases, others with wine bottles covered in spiderwebs. Amanda could feel Leah shiver beside her.

Slam!

The door to the cellar closed.

Leah gasped. "Now what? I told you it was a bad idea coming down here."

Amanda heard scratching. She swallowed and bit her lip. Her chest tightened. She didn't want Leah to know she was scared. What if there were rats in the cellar?

"Hold on. There must be a way to get upstairs." Amanda shone her phone around the room. "There, over there. I think that might be a door leading to the main floor."

Leah clung to Amanda's shoulder as they inched their way to the other side of the cellar. Amanda hoped the door didn't require another key. With a shaking hand, she turned the doorknob. The door swung open, revealing a set of steep stairs. The panting poodle almost knocked them over as it shot up the stairs. The girls followed and entered a dimly lit room at the top.

"Listen!" Amanda held her breath.

A long moan and a slurping sound came from nearby.

Leah walked over to a set of shutters and pulled them open. Sunlight from the backyard flooded the room, revealing Fifi licking the face of Philippe Lawrence, gagged and huddled in a corner.

15

AMANDA TOOK HER SWISS ARMY KNIFE OUT OF A POCKET IN her cargo pants and cut the ropes binding Philippe's arms and legs while Leah eased the duct tape from his mouth.

Philippe gasped and sputtered as he took in gulps of air. "Am I ever pleased to see the two of you." He rubbed his wrists. "How did you find me?"

Amanda gave the dog a pat on the head. "It was Fifi. She led us to you."

"But what happened to you? How did you get here in the first place?" asked Leah. "And whose house is this?"

Philippe held up his hands, palms out, to stop them. "I know, I know, lots of questions. But first, we should get out of here before someone comes back."

"The cellar door slammed shut, so we can't go back through the basement," said Amanda.

"Let's try the front door then." Philippe hobbled toward the front room, his limp more noticeable.

Leah shook her head. "We tried it from the outside and it was locked. We don't have a key."

They followed him through the dim powdery light to the front of the house. Beside the door hung a large old-fashioned key. Leah inserted it in the lock.

Click. The door opened.

"That's strange the key would be inside the house," said Amanda.

"It's often that way in these old French houses." With Fifi firmly in his arms, Philippe looked both ways as he led them out.

❈ ❈ ❈

Aunt Jenny was waiting for them at the gardens.

"Sorry we took so long, but I bought this hat." Leah pointed to her head. "And we found Mr. Lawrence."

"I see." Aunt Jenny peered at the man behind them with concern. "You don't look very well. Perhaps we should all have a cup of tea."

Over refreshments, the girls explained how they found Philippe.

"What happened?" asked Aunt Jenny, gently patting his hand.

"I was walking along with Fifi when someone hit me over the head. When I came to, I was in the old house the girls found me in."

"Did they take anything? Your wallet perhaps?"

He checked his pockets. "No, everything is here. Fifi must have run away and hid close to the house. She's a smart puppy to get your attention, Amanda. Thanks for following her and rescuing me. That was a brave thing to do." He nodded at Amanda and Leah, the colour returning to his face.

"Then why did they attack you?" asked Amanda. "Do you have any idea who did it?"

"I don't know." He shook his head and shrugged.

"Earlier we saw Aimee inside Monet's house. It's odd that everyone is here today."

"Aimee? Aimee was here?" Philippe looked confused as he rubbed his chin. He picked up Fifi. "I better get going. Thanks so much for rescuing me, girls. Be careful out there." He gave them a stern look, his bushy eyebrows meeting in the middle. "I wouldn't want anything bad to happen to you. Ms. Anderson, it was good to see you again. Keep an eye on these two." He limped away.

Aunt Jenny smiled faintly and collected her things. "I need to get back to Paris. Have you seen enough?"

"I'm ready to go," answered Amanda.

Leah adjusted her hat. "Me too."

After getting off the bus, they walked back to Shakespeare and Company. Along the way they spotted Pierre on the other side of the street. Amanda waved and he ran over to meet them.

"Hey, I was hoping to see you." Pierre's face lit up. "*Maman* is giving a cooking lesson on how to make macarons. She wondered if you would like to attend. It is at our apartment. Do you remember where it is? You can join as well, Madame Anderson."

"When?" asked Amanda.

"This afternoon at four o'clock. It will be good. You will be there, *non*?"

"Thanks. We'll try to be there." Aunt Jenny kept walking. Her phone pinged.

❀ ❀ ❀

The bookstore was quiet as Amanda dusted shelves. "You know what was odd? Philippe didn't seem very upset about being tied up."

"I don't believe a word he said." Leah straightened some books. "He's got lying eyes. I'm sure he knows who attacked him and why. He did seem surprised that Aimee was there too. Do you think . . . ?"

"No way! You don't think Aimee abducted him and tied him up?" Amanda stopped what she was doing and raised her eyebrows.

"I don't know but, Amanda, something doesn't add up." Leah shoved a book back in place. "And who slammed the door shut to the cellar?"

Fiona looked up from packing books in a box and labelling it. "Since it is so quiet, you girls can finish your shift. Aimee should be back soon."

"That's great," said Amanda. "We want to learn how to make macarons at Pierre's mother's place."

"Madame Duchamp is not only an accomplished artist, she is a great culinary artist as well."

Amanda looked at the address on the box. "Do you send books to Canada?"

"We send books all over the world. Our online bookshop is as busy as our physical store."

Just then, Aggie, the cat, jumped down from a shelf she had been sleeping on.

"Be careful you don't get packed in a box and sent to my place." Amanda stroked the fluffy white feline.

❋ ❋ ❋

They arrived at Pierre's apartment just on time. His mother, Yvette, was happy to see them again and gave them all hugs. She invited Amanda, Leah, and Aunt Jenny to join the others around the kitchen island.

She stood in front of the already measured-out ingredients. "Macarons are not difficult to make, but they can be tricky. There are some important things to remember." Yvette picked up an egg. "The eggs must be at room temperature. This is most important. I took these out of the fridge two hours ago." She cracked three eggs and emptied them into a pottery bowl. She then placed her hands in the bowl and scooped out the yolks. "We only need the whites for making macarons."

The girls enjoyed whipping the egg whites and later piping the rounds of dough onto a parchment-lined cookie sheet. While the cookies that made the base and top baked in the oven, the girls asked if they could see Yvette's pottery studio.

"But of course." Yvette motioned to Pierre. "Take the girls upstairs and put the lights on for them." Aunt Jenny stayed with the other guests as they discussed the history of French baking.

The studio, a loft lined with shelves overflowing with pots, glazes, boxes of pottery, and tools, smelled of earth and clay as well as oil paint and turpentine. An unfinished painting leaned on an easel in one corner. A bust of a bearded man with blank eyes rested on a column. Sketches littered the walls and rough clay animals were scattered on a table alongside an elaborate sculpture of fish and mermaids.

"Maman always has many projects on the go." Pierre chuckled.

The doorbell rang and Yvette shouted, "Pierre, *mon cher*, can you get that?"

"I better go. Stay and look around."

Amanda held up a tool that looked like a potato peeler. "She must use this to trim her sculptures." She saw movement out of the corner of her eye and froze.

Behind a decapitated statue lurked a young man in a black jacket.

"Jerome! Is that you? What are you doing here?"

16

JEROME STUFFED HIS HANDS IN THE POCKETS OF HIS JACKET and looked down at his shoes. "I-I'm just staying here for a while."

Leah narrowed her eyes. "What do you mean? Why can't you stay at your home?"

"It's complicated. Don't let on you know I'm here. Pierre's mum doesn't even know."

Pierre came up the stairs. "I see you found my stowaway. I mean my houseguest."

Amanda tilted her head to one side. "I didn't know you guys knew each other."

"We went to school together, here in Paris." Pierre spread out his hands, palms up. "He needed a place to hide out, so I said he could stay here. What are friends for, eh?"

"Who are you hiding from?" asked Amanda. "Not those same guys we saw in Versailles?"

Jerome looked away and shrugged.

"*Maman* said the macarons are ready to be assembled and sampled. We must get back downstairs. I will sneak some up to you later, Jerome." He winked and turned to go back downstairs.

"Are you going to be OK?" whispered Leah.

Jerome took a deep breath and looked away. "Yeah, I'll be fine." He somehow didn't look so tough as he gave a nervous smile.

"Should we ask Mr. Lawrence to help you?" asked Amanda.

Jerome stepped back. "No! Please don't tell him I'm here."

Pierre called from the bottom of the stairs, "Hurry, *mesdemoiselles*."

Amanda and Leah helped pipe butter cream filling onto each base and place another cookie on top to create delicate macarons. After everyone sampled their tasty creations, Yvette packed some for them to take home. They left behind the delicious sugar-and-almond smell of fresh-baked macarons and made their way back to the bookstore.

"That was fun," said Aunt Jenny, "and I met some interesting people too. Most of them are part of the artist community and interested in history. I think they may be able to assist me in my research. Tomorrow I have arranged to meet one couple at the Musée d'Orsay. Would you girls like to come with me?"

Leah scowled and shook her head. "I'd rather go shopping."

Amanda smiled. "I'd love to go to the museum. Pierre's mother said it was a great place with many amazing works of art."

"I said we would meet them in the morning before it gets too busy." Aunt Jenny glanced at Leah. "We can go shopping after."

＊＊＊

The next morning they arrived at what looked like an old train station.

"The Musée d'Orsay is housed in this train station," explained Aunt Jenny. "Would you believe it was scheduled to be demolished until the artist community asked the government to let them display a collection of art here? You will see it is the perfect location. Oh, there's the couple I'm supposed to meet." She waved at a man and woman standing by the front door.

Inside, marble sculptures lined the centre of the open space, basking in the sunlight coming through the high-domed glass ceiling. A massive clock hung on the wall above them at the entrance.

Aunt Jenny paid the admission, then gave the girls their tickets. "My friends and I are going up to the fifth floor to look at the Impressionist paintings first. You can come along if you wish or look through the display rooms on the ground floor. I'll meet you back here in one hour." She pointed to the clock. "You have your mobile, Leah, if you need me."

Amanda's eyes widened as she tried to take it all in. "I'd like to look around down here."

"Me too," said Leah.

Once Aunt Jenny left, Leah turned to Amanda. "I can't stop thinking of Jerome. It was so weird seeing him at Yvette's studio. Something's going on—I just can't figure out what."

"I was wondering the same thing." Amanda scratched her chin. "I can't help thinking he was involved in the fire at Notre-Dame and is worried he'll get caught."

"I don't think so." Leah shook her head. "I think he's afraid of the gang and your friend Mr. Lawrence. Maybe Jerome knows who started it. Like . . . maybe Philippe Lawrence?"

Amanda stared at her friend. "How can you even say that? He was part of the human chain removing the special items."

Leah placed her hands on her hips. "Amanda, he's shown up everywhere there's been a problem—at the Opera House, the Louvre, Notre-Dame, Versailles, and Giverny. I still think Aimee and him are up to no good."

"Maybe. Or maybe they're secret lovers. I just don't know what to think." Amanda sighed. "Let's look in this room."

They entered a room with a number of paintings displayed on the walls. Amanda gasped. "I can't believe this." She walked over to a painting of peasant women in a field, gathering wheat stalks. "This picture of The Gleaners is on a card my great-aunt Mary gave me. I love it so much, I have it tacked on the bulletin board in my bedroom. Now I'm seeing the picture in real life. This is incredible."

Leah peered closer. "It is a good painting. I wish I could paint like that. I'm rubbish at art. It's the only thing I always get a low mark in."

The museum wasn't very busy, so they had the room to

themselves. They went from painting to painting, talking about what they did and didn't like about each one. Others entered the room, but they didn't pay any attention.

Suddenly two boys stood close, one on each side of them. One boy grabbed Leah's wrist. The other held onto Amanda's arm with a firm grasp. Her muscles tightened as her heartbeat quickened and her stomach knotted.

"Where is Jerome?" growled the boy beside Leah.

"I don't know. Let—go—of—me," she shouted, trying to pull her hand away.

"Yes, you do, and you will tell me right now. Or we will hurt your little friend." He glared at Amanda while the other boy tightened his grip.

Just then a security guard entered the room. "What is going on in here?"

"We are just showing our little sisters the art, monsieur. They are learning about it in school."

The guard glanced at the boy's grip on Amanda's arm. The boy relaxed his hold. She jerked her hand away and stepped back.

"Let's go and find Aunt Jenny."

Leah swallowed. "Yes, she'll be expecting us."

The girls left the gallery, skirting around the security guard who glared at the boys. Hearts pounding, Amanda and Leah ran up the escalators two steps at a time, stopping at the top of each floor to quickly look and make sure no one followed them.

"Who were those guys?" asked Leah, catching her

breath, when they got to the fifth floor.

"I recognized the tattoo of a dragon on the boy's arm. He was one of the guys at Versailles that Jerome was trying to avoid."

"One of the boys from the gang?"

"Yes. I'm sure of it." Amanda scanned the room. "Now, where's Aunt Jenny?"

17

THE GIRLS LOOKED FOR AUNT JENNY AMONG THE PEOPLE viewing the artwork. They passed paintings of ballerinas, couples dancing, and picnics. At the end of the room was another enormous clock with large black hands and Roman numerals.

"Wow!" exclaimed Amanda. "You can look right through the clock to the outside. What an awesome view. And what's that shiny white domed building in the distance?"

"Oh, that. That's Sacré-Cœur, or Sacred Heart, a famous cathedral," answered Leah.

"Another one?"

"There are lots of them here. That one's not very old, though."

"I'd like to go there and see it."

"If you've seen one cathedral, you've seen them all." Leah smirked.

"That's so not true." Amanda stopped in her tracks. "They are all unique. Notre-Dame was amazing and not like any other I've seen. And now it's ruined." She fought back tears.

Leah looked at her sideways. "Well, I guess so. You seem to find something special wherever you visit. I'm just not like that." She put her arm around her friend. "They will rebuild Notre-Dame and it will be even better. We can visit it again in a few years." She gave her a reassuring squeeze.

Amanda nodded. "Paris is someplace I'll want to visit again."

"Oh, there you are." Aunt Jenny stepped around a corner. "I was about to go downstairs and find you. Should I take a picture of the two of you in front of the clock with Sacré-Cœur Cathedral in the background?"

"That would be awesome!" The girls stood in front of the huge clock, between the four and the five, arm in arm.

On the way out of the museum, Amanda noticed police officers talking to the two boys from the gang. One of the boys, his eyes narrowed, stared at her. Amanda hesitated before she crossed the street. She thought she saw Philippe Lawrence pull up in a car.

"Quickly, Amanda," Aunt Jenny yelled from the other side. "Cross the street before the light changes. The drivers here will not wait."

"*Arrêtez-vous!*" shouted a police officer.

Amanda froze. She knew that *arrêtez* meant stop. It was on some of the stop signs in Canada. She turned and looked at the officer, but he was pointing at Leah.

Leah turned crimson. "Me?"

"*Oui, toi,*" replied the officer who waved her over.

Leah and her aunt crossed back over the street with puzzled looks on their faces.

The police officer began speaking rapidly in French,

waving his arms about, pointing to the boys and then to Leah.

Philippe Lawrence stepped in, said something in French, and then turned to Leah. "Apparently, a call was made to these boys from your mobile phone. A call from Jerome Johnson, a young man the police are looking for. They want to see your phone. Do you have it with you?"

Leah pulled her phone from her back pocket and gingerly handed it over.

The police officer scrolled through her calls. He looked up and nodded, saying something in French.

"He will have to keep your phone," said Philippe.

"What is going on?" Leah blinked rapidly. "I—I haven't done anything wrong."

"Probably not, but you must cooperate. How did Jerome make a call from this phone? Did you leave it unattended at any point? Did it ever go missing?"

"Um, no. I—I don't think so."

"Look, she is just a child," said Aunt Jenny firmly. "She is not involved in anything to do with these boys. Can we just go now? You can keep the phone."

Mr. Lawrence turned to the officers and chatted for a few minutes. Then he announced to Aunt Jenny they could go, but they may need to be questioned later.

Aunt Jenny hailed a cab. Nobody said anything on the way back to the bookstore. Leah couldn't stop shaking, so Amanda held her hand.

When they entered the busy store, Leah ran past customers and straight up to the bedroom. Amanda followed close behind. Leah flung herself onto the bed.

"I hate it here," she sobbed. "And I hate Mr. Lawrence. Did you see how he treated me like a criminal? He's probably the criminal." She pounded her fists on the bed. "And he kept my phone! Is he even allowed to do that?"

"I thought he was very nice about it, actually," said Amanda. "And it was actually the police . . . "

"You would! Just leave me alone." Leah buried her head in her pillow.

Amanda sighed and went back downstairs.

Fiona spotted her and called her over. "Could you please put all these in this box?" She pointed to a stack of books.

"Where are they going?"

"We are delivering them to a youth hostel. Every month we donate slightly damaged books for the teenagers and young adults who have just come out of jail and need help finding jobs and places to live."

"Why were they in jail?"

"Sometimes they simply got involved with the wrong crowd. They just need to get on the right track."

Amanda thought for a minute. "Have you ever heard of people being tricked into joining gangs?"

Fiona nodded. "It's a big problem. Parents are busy working. Children are left alone and feel ignored. So they look for somewhere to belong and join a gang. Then they are asked to do bad things, like steal something. The kids do it to show they are worthy of belonging to the club. Later they are sorry they did it, but the gang members threaten to tell their parents. Then they are stuck in a bad situation."

"Do you think it might have been a gang that started the fire in Notre-Dame?"

Fiona shrugged. "You never know. By the way, have you seen Jerome Johnson around? His mother came here looking for him. She said he hasn't been at home or at work for a couple of days. She's quite worried."

Amanda swallowed. She was about to tell her that she had seen him and he was all right, when a customer called Fiona over to ask a question about a book.

Amanda finished packing the books and went back up to the bedroom. Leah sat cross-legged on the bed, filing her nails. She didn't look up but grunted at her.

18

"LEAH, WE NEED TO TELL JEROME'S MOM HE'S ALL RIGHT. She's worried about him."

"Really?" Leah put down her nail file and looked up.

"Yes, Fiona just told me."

Leah groaned. "I don't know what to do. I don't want to get him in trouble, but I do feel bad about his mom being worried."

Amanda tilted her head and looked at Leah. "What's going on? This is not like you to get involved with someone in trouble. Isn't that more like what I would do?" She raised her eyebrows.

"I know. Jerome came in here with his mom on the first day and we started talking. He comes across as being this tough guy, but he isn't really. He told me about this gang he was in and how they were against the establishment. He seemed excited about it all. Then a few things happened, and I thought maybe he was involved in the fire at the cathedral. Now he's trying to get away from the gang, but they won't let him."

"What about the call from your phone?"

"I lent him my phone. I thought he was calling Pierre to see if he could stay with him for a bit. I guess he phoned one of the gang."

Amanda sat on the edge of the bed and patted Leah's hand. "I see." She thought for a moment. "Well, we need to get him back to his mom's place or at least get a message to her that he's OK."

Aunt Jenny came up from downstairs. "Are you all right, Leah?"

"I'll be fine. I just wish Mr. Lawrence hadn't made me feel like a criminal."

"He was just doing his job."

"His job? He's an unemployed writer who goes busking to make some money."

Aunt Jenny glanced away and mumbled, "He helps the police sometimes with translating and such." She looked up and grinned. "I know. Let's go for lunch in Montmartre and see Sacré-Cœur up close. That will take your mind off all these unpleasant things. It's our second-last day. We should make the most of it."

"Sounds good!" Both girls jumped off the bed.

Amanda tore a page from her notebook and wrote something on it. On the way out of the bookstore, she slipped the note to Fiona. "Please get this to Jerome's mom."

❋ ❋ ❋

"Oh my! It looks like an ice cream cake." Amanda stared at the chalk-white towers of Sacré-Cœur glistening in the sun. On one side stood a bronze figure of Joan of Arc on a horse, looking very stalwart and brave.

"Look at the view of Paris from here." Leah pointed to the city sprawled out below them.

"This the highest point in Paris, so it's a great view," replied Aunt Jenny.

"I wonder how they keep the church so shiny and white," said Amanda.

"From what I've read about it, the stones used for its construction contain calcite, which acts like a bleach and makes the building beautiful and white when it gets wet. So every time it rains, it's as if it gets a new coat of paint." Aunt Jenny looked around. "I think there's a good restaurant near here where we can have lunch."

Wandering down delightful cobblestone streets lined with art galleries and bistros, dodging tourists talking and laughing and people walking their dogs, they came to a red building with a windmill on top.

"This is sooo cute!" Amanda exclaimed. "Can we eat here?"

"This is Moulin Rouge, a famous cabaret. It's not open for lunch, just evening shows." Aunt Jenny pointed across the street. "Over there is a cafe many famous writers used to frequent."

They had just settled down to look at the menu when Pierre came rushing in.

His eyes wide, he shouted, "I've been looking all over for you. Do you know where Jerome is?" He stopped to catch his breath.

"No!" both girls exclaimed.

"I thought he was . . . ouch."

Leah kicked Amanda's leg under the table. She realized Aunt Jenny didn't know that Jerome was hiding out at Pierre's place.

"I heard *la gendarmerie* took your phone, Leah. That's too bad. I am sure there has been a mistake."

"Would you like to join us for lunch?" asked Aunt Jenny.

"*Non, non, merci.* I must go to work. If you see Jerome, let me know."

Amanda and Leah exchanged looks of concern as he left the restaurant. Leah picked at her food.

They walked back through the charming streets. Aunt Jenny's eyes brightened as she shared her knowledge of the place. "Many well-known painters like Van Gogh, Renoir, and Pablo Picasso lived here, as it was quite affordable once. I lived here right after university. It was a fun place then, not as touristy." She sighed. "Let's go to Place du Tertre just behind Sacré-Cœur. You'll like that."

Amanda just wanted to look for Jerome. She sensed Leah felt the same because she kept twisting her hair around one finger.

"Sure," said Leah. "But then can we go back? I have a headache."

They entered a square with dozens of artists sitting under colourful umbrellas. In front of easels, they sketched and painted while people sat patiently waiting for their portraits to be completed.

"This looks like fun." Amanda watched a man with a

braided ponytail wearing a black beret paint a caricature of a small girl and her dog.

"Here you are, *pépette*." He handed the picture to the little girl.

She squealed with delight. "Momma, look. It is a picture of me."

The black poodle jumped off her lap, ran around the artist, and darted over to Amanda.

"Fifi! Is that you?" Amanda bent down to pat the dog's head.

She looked up just as the painter turned around. The artist was Philippe Lawrence.

19

"*Bonjour, mademoiselle.*" Philippe adjusted his beret and smoothed his beard. "Would you like your portrait painted?"

"Wh-what are you doing here! Are you an artist too?"

He winked. "I, my dear, am a man of many talents." Philippe lowered his voice. "It would be best if you pretend you don't know me." He picked up the dog and placed it in Amanda's arms. "You can have your portrait painted with *la petite chienne*, if you would like."

Aunt Jenny waved at Amanda from across the square. She pointed to Leah sitting on a stool smiling at a young illustrator as he sketched her. Amanda waved back and pointed to the canvas in front of Philippe.

Fifi squirmed in her arms. Amanda tried to keep her still by scratching behind her ears. Suddenly, the little dog barked and sprang off her lap. She ran around the easel, knocking it over. The poodle darted under a table and jumped over a stack of canvases, tipping over a pail filled with paint brushes, causing coloured water to splatter everywhere. Amanda raced around the busy square trying to catch her. Fifi darted between the feet of the many visitors and vendors.

Losing track of the dog, she stood with hands on hips and surveyed the scene, avoiding glares, shouts, and hand gestures from the artists. Out of the corner of her eye, she saw a flash of black enter a small alleyway and decided to follow it. Tall hedges guarded one side of the passageway and a large stone wall loomed on the other. The hairs on her arms stood on end as she made her way down the dark and gloomy passageway.

A young man stepped out from behind the hedge. She caught her breath.

"Are you looking for this?" In his arms he gripped a struggling black poodle.

Amanda's body tensed. "Leave her alone. She's just a puppy."

"I'll tell you what. I'll give you the dog after you tell me where Jerome is."

Amanda stood tall and crossed her arms. "What if I don't know where he is?"

"Oh, but I think you do." Smirking, he moved closer to her and grasped the dog tighter, exposing a dragon tattoo on his arm.

"*Yelp!*"

"Ouch." He dropped the dog and held his bleeding finger. "You little . . . "

Amanda scooped up Fifi and raced back the way she came. She bumped into Pierre as she entered Place du Tertre.

"Those boys, those boys from the gang are here. Th-they're looking for Jerome." Amanda stopped to catch her breath.

"I thought so," said Pierre. "Let us give Monsieur Lawrence his dog back. Then we must find Jerome."

"*Merci beaucoup*," said Philippe as he took the dog in his arms. "I will finish your portrait later, *mademoiselle*." He nodded and walked away as another person took his place in front of a blank canvas.

"Honestly, Amanda. One minute you're sitting getting your portrait done, and the next you're running around the square chasing a dog and causing mayhem. We can't leave you alone for a minute." Leah grinned and unrolled a piece of paper. "What do you think of my portrait?"

"Incredible! It looks like you, in a rock band."

"I know. I love it!" Leah glanced at Pierre. "I thought you had to go to work."

"I called to tell them I would be late. That something urgent came up."

"Where's Aunt Jenny?" Amanda glanced around.

"Over there." Leah pointed. "Talking to an artist she knew when she lived here."

Ping!

Pierre looked at his phone. "We must go to Père-La-chaise Cemetery. Jerome has been spotted there by a friend. I believe he is in great danger."

When they asked Aunt Jenny if they could go to the cemetery, she was delighted. "It's one of my favourite places in Paris. I used to hang out there with my friends. But why the urgency?"

"I need to find a person who needs my help," replied Pierre.

They took the Metro to the cemetery. Aunt Jenny explained they were going to the largest and most visited graveyard in Paris, where over one million people were buried, including some famous people.

"Like who?" asked Amanda.

"Frederic Chopin, Oscar Wilde, Edith Piaf, and Jim Morrison from the American rock group, the Doors," replied Aunt Jenny.

"I've heard of him. My dad has a book about him and likes his music."

"So does mine." Leah shrugged. "I bet you're going to love this place. What is it with you and graveyards anyway?"

"Here's our stop," shouted Pierre.

They approached an imposing stone gateway and entered through a green door between two tall pillars. Amanda gasped as they stepped into a lush garden with graves lining a myriad of cobblestone paths. It looked like a village of tombs, with tiny houses and mini castles crowded together. Many of the grave markers were decorated with ornate carvings. A stone piano stood on the tomb of a musician. On top of a large granite stone was the statue of a painter wearing a beret and holding a palette.

Although there were many people visiting, it felt very peaceful. Amanda stopped and gazed at the scene before her. "This is the most amazing cemetery I have ever seen."

Pierre looked from left to right. "I wonder where Jerome

is." His phone pinged. "We need to go to Jim Morrison's grave. Follow me."

"This place is massive. How do you know where it is?" asked Leah.

"I used to do tours here." Pierre picked up the pace.

"I need to stop at Oscar Wilde's final resting place. I'll catch you up," said Aunt Jenny as they neared a monument covered with lipstick kisses.

They arrived at the grave of Jim Morrison. Fans had left flowers and personal mementos, but there was no sign of Jerome. As they were about to leave, Amanda spotted a shadow move between the tombstones. "I'll just be a minute." She left the group to investigate.

Before she knew it, someone reached out and pulled her behind a large stone. She opened her mouth to scream, but a hand clamped it shut.

20

"Don't be afraid. It's just me," whispered a voice she recognized. "I need you to be very quiet and to trust me. Do you promise not to scream?"

Amanda nodded. Philippe Lawrence removed his hand and pointed. Between two monuments crouched Jerome. Amanda gasped then covered her mouth. Two boys crept through the gravestones, looking behind each one and parting the surrounding bushes. Jerome, looking in the opposite direction, didn't see them.

"I have to warn him," whispered Amanda.

Phillippe hesitated. "OK. But be careful."

Amanda picked her way around a cherub-topped stone. She lost sight of Jerome and could hear Leah and Pierre call her name. Her muscles tensed as she narrowed her eyes and peered into a dim corner. Her foot caught on an exposed tree root. She fell forward and hit the side of a gravestone. Everything went black.

✤ ✤ ✤

"Is she alive?"

Someone touched her wrist.

"I think so. She has a pulse."

99

Amanda opened her eyes slightly but only glimpsed a fuzzy dragon tattoo before they closed again. The voices sounded far away.

"What should we do with her?"

"We can't leave her here. If she dies we could be accused of murder. We're in enough trouble already."

Through a fog, Amanda heard a familiar voice. "You'd better not leave her here to die."

"Jerome, we've been looking for you. You disappeared. That's not a good thing to do, man."

"I'm finished with you lot. The police are looking for you. They think you have something to do with the fire in the cathedral."

"Hey, we had nothing to do with that. We already cleared it up with *la gendarmerie*. You owe us a job."

"Look, I did what you asked. I made the call of a bomb at the Opera House. I got rid of Mr. Lawrence in Giverny and messed with the lights in the Louvre. Now I'm done. I don't want to be part of your gang anymore."

Amanda heard scuffling and shouting.

"Right! All of you are under arrest. Don't even think of leaving. The police are waiting outside the gates. But first we have to get Amanda looked after."

Amanda opened her eyes and saw Philippe handcuff the two boys from the gang.

He glanced at Jerome. "I won't cuff you as long as you promise not to run."

Jerome nodded and bent down to help Amanda up.

"You OK?"

She moaned and held her head. "My head hurts, but I think I'm all right."

"You'll probably have a big lump there tomorrow."

While they helped her to the walkway, Philippe shouted, "Leah, Jenny, over here."

Leah screamed when she saw them. "What have you done to Amanda? If you've hurt her, I'll kill you, you horrible man." She ran at Philippe with her fists up.

Jerome restrained her. "It's all right, Leah. He didn't hurt her. She tripped and fell against a gravestone."

"That's true." Amanda gave a weak smile.

"Take her someplace to sit down for a few minutes. I have something I need to do." Philippe put his cell phone to his ear.

Soon Aimee arrived with two police officers who took the scowling boys from the gang away. "*Merci*, Monsieur Lawrence," said one officer as they passed by.

"How are you, Amanda? Do you need me to take you to the hospital?" asked Aimee.

"I'm feeling better, thanks. Pierre gave me some water. I don't want to go to the hospital."

"We'll keep an eye on her," replied Aunt Jenny.

Philippe turned to Jerome. "What should we do with you?"

"I'm willing to cooperate. I'm so done with gangs."

"Good, that will be in your favour."

Amanda squinted at Mr. Lawrence. "You're not just a

writer-artist-busker, are you?"

Philippe shrugged. "I guess I better own up. I'm an undercover police officer with Scotland Yard working with Europol to break up this and other gangs."

Amanda's mouth fell open. For once she had no words.

❋ ❋ ❋

The next day Pierre took the girls up to the top of the Eiffel Tower.

"Wowza! What an amazing view. I feel like I'm on top of the world." Amanda took pictures of the city below them and then selfies of herself and Leah.

Aunt Jenny, Philippe, and Aimee waited for them at the bottom of the tower.

Philippe Lawrence grinned. "Everything is sorted out. The gang has been disbanded and will not be causing any more trouble. Jerome was a big help and will be doing community service work for the next few months. He asked me to thank you, Amanda, for letting his mother know he was all right and staying at Pierre's place."

He smiled at Aimee. "Aimee has been assisting me with this case. She's studying criminology at university and this was part of her work experience. She will make a great police officer one day. And thank you, Jenny, for your assistance. Your research skills came in handy."

Aunt Jenny blushed as he shook her hand, placing his other hand on top of hers. "So sorry about looking through your research books in the room. I was just curious about what you were researching and if you would be able to help me."

"But—but who started the fire in the cathedral?" asked Amanda.

"They still don't know, but it is suspected that the fire may have been accidentally started as a result of some of the reconstruction work," explained Philippe. "We may never know for sure." He handed Amanda a flat square package. "I believe I owe you this."

She opened it and placed her hand on her heart. Inside was a painting of Amanda, wearing a suit of armour, sitting on a horse. She turned it over. On the back was written, "To Amanda, as brave as Joan of Arc." It was signed P Lawrence. "Thank you so much. I just love it." She gave Philippe a hug.

Pierre walked back with them to the bookstore, where they picked up their already packed bags. Amanda handed a copy of her essay to Fiona just before they left.

"Thanks for all the work you did for us while you stayed here," said Fiona. "I truly believe you will be a published author one day. Your picture may hang on our wall of fame." She gave Amanda a vintage copy of *Anne of Green Gables*. "Come back any time."

"I will treasure this forever!" Tears formed in Amanda's eyes.

Leah and Aunt Jenny smiled with pride.

Pierre lifted her hand and kissed it like Prince Charming. "*Adieu, mademoiselle.*"

Amanda giggled with delight.

Aggie, the cat, rubbed against her leg and purred.

❋ ❋ ❋

On the way to the airport, Leah confessed, "I was wrong about Philippe Lawrence. I'm sorry."

"That's OK. I was wrong about Jerome, sort of." Amanda smirked then got serious. "Should we still travel? What with terrorists, bombs going off, and all that scary stuff."

Leah thought for a moment. "I was thinking about that too. But if we all stop travelling, won't that be like letting the bad guys win?"

"I agree. There are so many more places I want to visit. I know I want to come back to Paris, the city of love, one day. After all, I will need to see the reconstructed Notre-Dame Cathedral."

DISCUSSION QUESTIONS

1. Would you like to visit Paris? Why?

2. Are you familiar with Claude Monet's paintings? Which one is your favourite?

3. Would you like to sleep in a bookstore in exchange for volunteer work?

4. Amanda doesn't think she is very brave. Do you think she is brave? Why?

5. If you visited France, what site would you most like to see?

6. What French king built the Palace of Versailles?

7. Do you think people should stop travelling because of the threat of terrorists?

8. Where do you think Amanda should go next? Why?

ACKNOWLEDGEMENTS

I have many people to thank for their support, advice, and suggestions that enabled this story to come to life. My dream to visit the romantic city of Paris came true when we took our dog on a road trip to visit friends living on the outskirts of the city. Paris, and the surrounding area, was everything I imagined it to be and more. So, the first people I wish to thank are Alain and Catherine Marsan who were the very best hosts. They took the time to show us around the city as well as Versailles and Giverny, treated us to amazing French cuisine, and proudly shared their love of this incredible part of the world. I knew immediately that Amanda had to visit France. What I didn't know at the time was that there would be a terrible fire in Notre Dame one year after my visit. This upsetting event became the basis of my story.

As always, I could not have created this adventure without the help of my critique groups in Canada and Spain. Their ability to notice details and suggestions to improve the writing has been invaluable. A huge thank you goes to Molly Ringle for her expert editing skills that put the finishing touches on the story. I also want to thank my publisher, Michelle Halket of Central Avenue Publishing, for once again producing a book I am proud of.

Thank you to my beta readers including Maureen Moss for ensuring the French words were used correctly, Marion Iberg for her razor-sharp eye for detail, and Sheila MacArthur for ensuring the story flowed. To my street team of middle-graders, thank you for being you and giving me ideas and suggestions along the way. You help keep my stories fresh and current.

Most importantly, thank you to all the Amanda fans who keep asking for more adventures!

ABOUT THE AUTHOR

Photo: K. Cullen

Brought up on a ranch in southern Alberta, Darlene Foster dreamt of writing, travelling the world, and meeting interesting people. She believes everyone is capable of making their dreams come true. It's no surprise that she's now the award-winning author of a children's adventure series about a travelling twelve-year-old girl.

A world-traveller herself, Darlene spends her time in Vancouver, Canada, and Costa Blanca in Spain with her husband and her amusing dogs, Dot and Lia.

darlenefoster.ca

@supermegawoman